THE WIFE HE PROTECTED

Clearwater Romance Book Four

MEGAN MCCOY

Published by Blushing Books
An Imprint of
ABCD Graphics and Design, Inc.
A Virginia Corporation
977 Seminole Trail #233
Charlottesville, VA 22901

Megan McCoy
The Wife He Protected

EBook ISBN: 978-1-64563-914-5
Print ISBN: 978-1-64563-915-2
v1

Chapter 1

Beth Sinclair walked out her front door into the warm spring air. The breeze smelled of flowers and trees, and just freshness on this lovely May day in Clearwater so walking she would go. She'd been cooped up in her home office too long. Downtown was only six blocks away and there were no sweets in the house. Something that needed remedied, badly. Today was Friday and their entire weekend loomed ahead. Her sister, Joni had said something about grilling out after she got home from work today, so the least she could do was supply dessert. Luckily, she only worked half days on Friday, so she had time to walk downtown and grab a dessert from Jordyn's shop. Joni would be home by the time she got back, which was nice. Beth didn't really mind being home alone, but didn't like coming back into an empty house.

Walking, she kept looking around, keeping a watchful eye out, while she strolled through the quiet neighborhood. She loved living in Clearwater. It wasn't her old life, but it was a safe, happy life. Doing what she wanted when she wanted and what she felt safe doing with no one fussing over her except her sister now and then, was a wonderful thing. It had been almost three years now since they'd moved here, and even she felt safe now in this sweet little town. Cautious but safe. They'd made a good move to their grandmother's old house that they had slowly made into their own.

Beth arrived at the downtown square and headed to Jordyn's shop. As she always did, she stopped and looked up at the sign she'd designed for Jordyn's bakery, Baking Memories. It always filled her with nostalgia. Almost like homesickness.

Being a graphic designer had been her passion and she'd been good at it. Really good. But then, well, it had just felt good to finally do it again. The insurance company paid her very well, and the hours were excellent. Still she missed designing now and then, and the craving was getting stronger to get back to it. She'd done some brochures and flyers and things for her friend Ellie, but those didn't satisfy her much. Feeling the need to stretch her creative wings kept getting stronger. There was the fact, though, she knew she couldn't go back to her old life.

Sighing, she walked in the door of the shop, thinking while she enjoyed her company, Ellie wasn't really her friend. She was Joni's friend and they allowed her to hang out sometimes. Did it matter? It was starting to, but right now, she needed cupcakes.

"Beth!" Jordyn called out from behind the display case. "Good to see you!"

"Hello, Jordyn," Beth said. "How's business?"

"Exceeding expectations," she said, and looked around. Then lowered her voice and held out her hand. "Look!"

Beth looked at the sparkling ring Jordyn was flashing. "Are you and Ben engaged?"

Jordyn nodded. "You are the first person I told! Other than my mom and she didn't understand, but, well, it felt right to tell her. I'm telling my sister tomorrow then announcing to the friends with a small dinner party."

Beth smiled but felt a pang. Joni would be one of those friends. She would not be. The party would probably consist of Joni, Ellie, Lucy, Izzy, and a few others, but not her. "I won't tell a soul! Congratulations! I'm so happy for you!"

"Thank you," Jordyn all but beamed she seemed so happy. "I can't believe I get to marry my mountain man."

"You were made for each other," Beth said, suddenly tired of the conversation. "Can you give me a dozen Aunt Daisy's oatmeal cookies and a half dozen each of triple chocolate brownie cupcakes, and strawberry cheesecake bites?"

It was less than five minutes before she was out the door, with her box of goodies, into the fresh summer air. For some reason, she'd felt as if she had been suffocating in there.

Beth headed home, pondering her life. Was this it? Forever? Just being home and working from home, with an occasional foray into town. No real friends, no real relationships but her sister? Everyone else thought of her as Joni's reclusive sister, if they thought of her at all and Beth suspected that mostly they didn't. Heck, she even had to borrow Joni's car if she wanted to go anywhere.

Blending and not being noticed was a good thing when they had moved here. A few years later, though, well, it was starting to get to her. She needed to be with people. Get out of the house. Make some friends of her own. Be whatever it was that passed for normal. Go out to eat. Date.

Beth shook her head, not believing she was actually thinking about dating. But she was and that was normal. Normal. That word kept coming up a lot in her mind lately. Was she ready to be normal instead of, well, what she had been for the last few years? She thought she might be ready. Did she need to wait till she was really ready?

Maybe she'd let her hair go back to her natural color instead of this mousy brown. Grow it down to her waist again, if she could. Find a job in her chosen field of work.

Or maybe not. Nothing had to happen immediately, after all.

Beth sighed and turned down her street. One thing, for certain though, she did love this old house. It had been their grandmother's and she'd left it to her and her two sisters. Sitting empty for a few years, Ellie, who had been a realtor before she turned into a hot shot city manager with political aspirations, had helped them get everything ready before they came down to move in. Sydney, their younger sister, had even moved here for a few months before she left for Chicago to go to vet school. Syd often wondered if their mom, a busy pediatric surgeon even noticed she'd left home. She needed to call Sydney tonight, it had been a while since they'd talked. Their mom? Well, she'd call when she had the time.

Walking in the front door, she heard music out on the back deck they'd built last year, tearing down the old porch where she and her sisters and their cousins had spent many a long summer afternoon playing. Termites decided it was time for it to go though. There was a time for everything, Beth knew, and felt change was coming. Right now, though, she wanted supper. Joni must have gotten home a little early and she was glad. Had she eaten today? She didn't remember.

"Joni, I'm home!" she called. "I brought dessert!" Putting the box on the table, she headed to the back door, they'd changed from a banging screen door to glass French doors.

Stopping short, she heard Joni scream from the backyard, "Beth! Call 911! Now!" Beth suddenly couldn't breathe. Was this it? Should she help Joni or hide? She felt frozen and as if all the blood had left her body. "Now, Beth! Hurry!"

Hitting 911, Beth made a decision and hurried to the patio to save her sister and almost sagged with relief seeing a fire. It was a fire. She saw Joni fanning the flames for some reason and Hank running over from the house next door.

"This is 911, what is the address of your emergency?" a

voice said. Beth gave the address and said, "Fire in the backyard. It's gotten out of control."

She hung up and stuck the phone in her pocket, racing back to the kitchen for the fire extinguisher. By the time she got it and got back out, Hank had the garden hose on, and was spraying the fire out. She set the fire extinguisher down and watched him, trying not to tremble. Slowing her breathing, she watched, as if it were a slow motion movie while her sister and the neighbor ran around with the hose putting the fire out. Why did it look so odd? It felt as if they were characters in a movie and she was way up on the balcony, peering down.

Beth noticed in a strange, odd little part of her brain that the firepeople showed up. Fire people? She wondered, and also wondered what happened to her slow calm breathing. It just seemed to leave, along with coherent thoughts. Luckily, her ears were ringing so loudly the only thing she could hear was her sister screaming, "Beth! Call 911. Now!" It wouldn't stop. It wouldn't stop. She sank down beside the fire extinguisher and tried to focus on the strong buzzing in her ears instead. Her vision seemed to be getting dark. What was going on? Smoke inhalation? Why did she feel so strange?

Maybe she'd just take a little nap? There were miniature people running all over her yard and there was nothing she could do. Besides, the ringing was getting louder. Her head felt as if it were floating away and she decided to go with it. Why not? Who would care? Finally her eyes closed and the strange people went away.

"Beth? Beth? Hey, open your eyes. Good girl. Hi, Beth, my name is Nick. Welcome back. How are you doing?"

Beth opened her eyes, wondering where she was and what happened, but saw the bluest eyes she'd ever seen and stopped wondering. Or caring.

"There you are," the voice that belonged to the eyes said. "Can you talk to me?"

Could she? Who knew? She shut her eyes again.

"Nope, don't do that. Stay with me. Beth. Open your eyes. Come on, right now."

She fluttered her eyes open again to see if his eyes really were that color. They sure were.

"Did you hit your head?"

Did she? She was lying down, which she didn't remember doing. No, she didn't hit her head. She didn't think so anyway. "Answer me, Beth." The tone was an amazing mix of gentle and stern. She liked it. It felt comforting, like he would take care of her. That was ridiculous.

"No," she said, and thought she should try to sit up. His hands were on her head and his fingers felt amazing. A nice scalp massage would feel really good, especially with his fingers. "No. I just got lightheaded."

Joni appeared to the side of her. "Beth, I'm so so sorry. I wasn't thinking. I didn't mean to scare you. Are you all right?"

"Yeah, I'm okay." This time she managed to move a little to try and sit up.

"Can you get her some water?" Nick asked.

Sure, she'd get up and get some water. For who? Joni? Oh, he meant for her, of course. She was the one who, who what?

"What happened?" she asked those blue eyes.

"You seem to have passed out," he said. "Have you eaten today?"

"I don't remember," she said. "Joni was going to grill out." She let him help her sit up, because why not. It wasn't like she'd been sitting up alone since she was six months old or anything. Joni came back with the water, and he handed it to her. "Drink up," he said, and it felt like a comforting command that didn't bother her at all for some reason. Obediently she put the bottle to her lips and took a few swallows. Why? Because he'd told her to, of course.

Hank came up from behind. "They said it's all out and everything is safe. Joni, what happened?"

"It was an accident, Hank! Accidents happen. I bumped into the grill and knocked it over." Joni sounded very defensive, Beth thought. Why? Accidents did happen.

"I've told you for months now that grill wasn't safe and that leg was going. Listening to me would be a good thing." Hank sounded annoyed. Beth hadn't realized their grill was unsafe. "I'm taking you to the store right now and we're getting you a new one."

"No," Joni said. "I don't need you to do that."

Hank shook his head. "Wasn't a question, a statement of fact. I'm not going to have either one of you burning down my fence or my garden."

"Oh, well, as long as it's all about you." They glared at each other and Beth saw Nick smile. His eyes weren't the only handsome thing about him. He had a small dark beard, an absolutely gorgeous nose and those cheekbones. Perfect teeth and a full head of dark hair that was a little longer than the usual fashion but seemed to fit him.

She couldn't help but smile back at him. Being used to Joni and Hank, their bickering and on and off again relationship was amusing at times. Other times it was simply annoying.

"Beth, are you okay?" Nick asked her as if they were friends or something. "Do you want to go to the emergency room and get checked out?"

She shook her head. "I didn't hit my head or anything, just got a little lightheaded."

"I scared her," Joni said. "It's my fault. Yes, Henry, it's all my fault, the fire, scaring Beth, all of it. Bethie, are you okay for real? I'm so sorry."

"It's okay," Beth assured her as Nick helped her to her feet.

"See, I'm fine. Just, well, you know." It had been a long time since a man had touched her. It felt right, somehow.

Joni nodded and hugged her, whispering, "I'm so sorry."

Nick said, "Okay, the guys are waiting on me. I'll go now, but if you need anything give us a call." He smiled at her again and reached over to pat her arm and suddenly that felt like a very intimate move. *Beth, girl, you do need a date*, she thought.

"Thank you," she told him. "I appreciate it."

"We aim to please," he said, and headed off the porch around to the front of the house, and Beth watched him go, feeling some kind of weird feeling. Abandonment? Bereft? Something. Why did she want to run after him? She didn't, she didn't even know him. He could be a serial killer for all she knew. He very easily could be. They could be very handsome and charming after all, and even have electric blue eyes.

"Come on, Beth. I'm making you a sandwich and a bowl of soup and then Hank and I are going to buy a new grill. If you are okay alone for a while?"

"I'll be fine, Joni," Beth said, dragging her eyes away from the spot she'd last seen Nick. "I can even make my own soup and sandwich."

Hank shook his head. "Not happening, Beth. Come on, we need to make sure you're okay and fed before we go."

Whatever. Did it matter? She knew why she passed out and it had nothing to do with lack of food and everything to do with shock. If she never heard 'call 911' again, it would be too soon. However, there was that firefighter with the blue eyes.

No one was worth setting your house on fire for, she reminded herself as she sat down in the comfortable kitchen. This was her favorite room in the house, with her Grandma's old sewing room, now turned into her office, a close second. Her office was a very small little room with no windows, unlike this room that had enough to let all the light in. The big sunny kitchen window overlooked what used to be her grandmother's herb garden that Joni was trying to whip into some kind of shape. After a few years of Joni's work though, it was still a tangle of weeds and flowers, much to next door neighbor Hank's dismay.

However, she felt safe in her office. She'd installed a reinforced door and two deadbolts along with a sturdy lock. It was almost like her little safe room. She always kept a burner phone in there, plus had her computer and ball bat, and a container of pepper spray. It was more than likely a waste of money, but the peace of mind made her feel much safer in the entire house, not only in that room where she worked forty or more hours a week. This room made her happy though. They hadn't remodeled much in here. Joni had painted, they'd bought new countertops and had them installed, they'd pulled up the old linoleum and put down a manufactured hard wood that looked real, but the old oak cabinets were still in good shape, the huge farmhouse sink was back in style again, and the windows always sparkled behind the cheery red and white checked curtains. The French doors, with their reinforced glass windows overlooked the deck and backyard. Plus it often just smelled good in here, cookies or bread, or whatever was in the oven for supper. She liked to cook and Joni was learning to bake bread thanks to Hank who had to be the best bread baker in Clearwater. But there wasn't much Hank couldn't do. He taught school, coached middle school ball, had a fantastic garden filled with flowers, herbs and veggies. And he also baked. The only thing it seemed he couldn't do, was get along with Joni for more than a few days or weeks at a time. She'd never seen two people who broke up and got back together more than those two. He'd probably be her brother-in-law one day and she'd be the one Joni would come running to after their fights.

Beth sat passively and watched as Joni popped open a can of soup they'd canned the summer before, dumped it in a bowl and stuck it in the microwave. Then she got out the bread, butter, peanut butter and jelly. Beth smiled. Fried peanut butter and jelly, their mom's go to when they got sick. Other kids got tomato soup and grilled cheese. They got vegetable soup and fried peanut butter and jelly. It was funny how they reverted when they were stressed.

"So are you really okay?" Joni asked Beth as she put down a glass of sweet tea in front of her. "Drink."

Beth nodded her head, and glanced at Hank, but she'd figured out a long time ago, he probably already knew everything. "I am. Just hearing you yelling to call 911, well, you know."

Joni nodded and came over to pat her arm. "I wasn't thinking. I just panicked about the fire. I'm so so sorry."

"I was glad to see it was a fire," Beth said. "You know."

"I do know," Joni said, flipping over the sandwich to brown on the other side, then taking the soup out of the microwave and putting it in front of her. "Eat, sandwich will be done in a minute."

Beth picked up her spoon and looked at Hank. "Why don't you guys go ahead to the store and get the grill before it gets too late? I'm fine, really. Thank you, Joni." She moved the offered sandwich over to her and took a bite of soup. It was just as good as it had been fresh last summer, bursting with flavors that had grown in their, or Hank's, garden. He and Joni were a good gardening team. His yard was just like a picture in a magazine. Their's wasn't yet, but was getting better. Except for that herb garden that frustrated Joni so much.

"You eat a few bites first, okay? I want to make sure you eat."

Beth tried not to roll her eyes. "I eat, I just was waiting on supper today to eat. I got busy."

"You need to not do that. You're allowed to eat more than once a day," Joni scolded.

"I brought cupcakes and things for dessert," Beth said, changing the subject. "I think I got enough for the weekend."

"How's Jordyn?" Joni seemed to allow herself to change the subject. "I haven't seen her in a while. She's so busy with the shop and Ben. I don't think I've seen her since we helped her move into her apartment a few months ago."

"She mentioned she wanted to get together with you all soon, and seemed good," Beth said. She, of course, hadn't been invited to help Jordyn move. That had been for 'the friends', of course. Once again, she felt the need to branch out a little, and make some friends of her own. She was way too old to be Joni's little tag along sister. Or to be babysat. They'd been here three years now, almost. Things were safe, and fine. She didn't need to hide like a little scaredy cat. Anymore, at least. "Busy, of course." She almost told her about the ring, but why ruin a good surprise? Unlike her, Joni loved a surprise. She preferred her quiet, calm, stable life. The life she'd been getting a little tired of recently. Not tired enough to do much of anything about it, yet, though. Just enough to angst over it some.

"Bethie, why don't you go to the hardware store with us? You could look for canning lids and explore that little gift nook you like so much."

"I can be alone for an hour, Joni," Beth said, and put another bite of sandwich in her mouth to not say anything more. She couldn't blame Joni for hovering, especially after what just happened.

"I don't know. I feel bad about leaving you." Joni looked over at Hank who shrugged as if to say, up to you.

"Well, feel bad or don't feel bad, but I'm not going, and you are. We can have cookies and cupcakes tonight while we watch *"Independence Day"* again. You've been looking forward to movie night." Joni did love her action adventure movies. Since she preferred horrible D list movies where a huge unstoppable monster terrorized the world, this one was a good compromise. One they both liked.

Hank shook his head. "You girls and your chick flicks."

"We can't all adore subtitled foreign films," Beth teased him. "You are the high brow intellect around here."

Hank curled his fingers, blew on them and rubbed them on his shirt. "What can I say? Tough job but someone has to do it."

"As long as I don't have to watch them," Joni teased, while yawning loudly. "I mean, unless I'm really tired and need a nap."

"Yeah, but then your snoring makes it hard to hear," Hank told her.

"Henry!" she complained.

"Hey, you two take your bickering to the store and get us a new grill. Let me eat in peace." She took another bite and stared at them while they stood up.

"Got your phone, Beth?" Joni asked. "I have mine. Just call if you need me."

"Yes, Mommy," Beth said, and smiled. "I promise. I'll probably go back to my office for a while. Ellie has flyers she wants designed for some event she's working on."

"Of course she does," Hank agreed. "Come on, Joni. Let's take our bickering to the hardware store so I can put the grill together before it gets dark."

Joni stood up but seemed reluctant and threw Beth a look. "Go!" Beth told her. "I want a cupcake and I'll be waiting for you!"

"Okay. Just call, though, okay?"

"Joni," Beth warned. "Go."

She watched them go out the back door, probably to cut through the backyard and take Hank's truck. What kind of grill would they come home with? She and Joni had a small charcoal one, and speaking of that, she should go out and clean up all the charcoal and see what kind of damage the fire had caused to the yard. She hoped it didn't get to the roses and thank goodness it didn't get to the house or the fencing. Grass could be replaced. Well, technically the house and fence could be, too, but not as easily. Especially when you lived next door to a Master Gardner who cherished his picture perfect lawn and gardens.

After she rinsed her dishes, she grabbed some leather gloves from the junk drawer and headed outside. There was a metal can in the garage in case anything was still hot. She looked at the small grill, still dripping water and foam from the firefighter's extinguisher since hers didn't get used. Yeah, one leg had broken completely off. Rusted through? She really couldn't tell, but how had neither she nor Joni seen that and fixed or tossed it? Luckily, nothing bad had really happened.

Shaking her head, she opened the garage and got the metal can, and went back out. When had she gotten to be such a wimp? She remembered the strong, confident, yes, even popular person she'd been before. That woman would never have fainted. She would have taken charge and managed things. Handled it and probably laughed about it, instead of panicking. At least she'd only fainted instead of having a full blown panic attack. It had been, what? Well over six months since she had one. That was a very good sign, wasn't it? Of course it was. Another sign.

It didn't take long for her to get everything cleaned up, and the grass didn't look too bad. Probably be able to tell more in the next day or so, though. Carefully, she made sure the metal can was far away from both the garage and the house in case something simmered in there and decided to come to a full boil later on.

Simmering? Yeah, she could feel her anxiety simmer

under the surface and decided a good idea would be to go to her office for a while, till Joni got home. It was a lovely, lovely, May afternoon though. It wouldn't be dark for a few hours yet. Staying outside felt tempting, but she'd already had one issue today. Another one would not be fun.

Going back in the house, she locked the back door, and double checked the front one, and then went to her office, closing and locking the door. There. All nice and cozy in her own personal little jail cell.

"Fun times, Beth," she muttered to herself and she pulled up the design program on her computer. There were flyers to design before she could break out of here.

She put today out of her head. Tomorrow would be a better day, and there would be cupcakes and cheesecake bites tonight. Life was good, she reminded herself.

Then she paused, picked up her phone and texted Ellie. "Ellie, this is Beth. My schedule suddenly freed up, and I'd love to help at the fundraiser this weekend. Just let me know where you need me."

She put her phone down and tried to calm the hammering in her heart. This was a good thing. She'd be safe in a crowd of people while she worked a booth and it was step one to getting back in the real world. Otherwise, she might as well be like Jordyn's mom, in a nursing home and lost in her own mind. She was too young for that and that first step had to come sometime.

"Great! Will text you details later!" Ellie responded.

And so she was committed.

"So, Nick, what about the hot little brunette?" Xavier asked as they washed down the truck.

"You know I like redheads," Nick said. "I like a little spice in my women."

"Hair color can be changed," Paige reminded him from where she was checking the medical kits.

"Well, considering what I do for a living, someone so afraid of fire they pass out, wouldn't be a good fit," he told them.

"But, but! Your biological clock!" Paige teased, stashing the bag back in the truck. "Time's running out!"

"For you, maybe," he said. "Me, I can have kids till I'm eighty."

"And they could all fight over who gets to push your walker," Xavier said.

"As long as they don't push it down the stairs," Paige added. "You gotta watch out for that. Your kids would be feisty."

"I'm not that rich or that grouchy," Nick told them. "They'd be nice to me."

"Yeah," Xavier said. "I have teenagers. You just keep telling yourself that."

"Don't scare the man off!" Paige said. "He'll be a great dad. You know, if he can ever find someone who will put up with him, but really, he's too picky. He's doomed to be alone forever."

"Doomed is a strong word," Nick protested as he finished up. "Shift is almost over. You all have plans?" While he loved his job, what he also loved was his schedule. They worked four twelve hour days followed by four days off. It meant his days off changed all the time, and holidays were often on the schedule, but overall, it was great to have that long stretch of time off.

"Maybe you should make a house call and go see the hot fainting lady?" Xavier suggested. "Just to make sure she's okay."

Nick shook his head. "Not my type. I've actually promised to work the kids' firehouse at some event down at the square Saturday. Then I'm probably going fishing."

"Yeah, you won't find a girl there," Paige said.

"You never know," Nick said, opening his locker and grabbing his stuff. "I'm outta here. See you all same time, same place next week."

"We will be here, have fun!"

Nick walked out and got in his truck to head home. He did love his job, but it was great to have a few days off to recharge. It was Thursday night and he didn't have to be at work till 6 a.m. Tuesday morning. He loved this little town, his new hometown, and most of the people in it. As towns went, this one had a lot going for it which helped make his decision to move here, well, that and the job offer that had come with a nice raise from where he'd been working. There was little crime, and the houses were inexpensive and the lake fantastic. He bought a little bass boat last year and spent a lot of time out there, fishing or cruising the lake or sometimes taking a pretty thing to a secluded cove and doing what came naturally. Why was he thinking of the skittish little brunette in the baggy jeans and oversized shirt he'd seen earlier today? She wasn't his type. His type was a feisty, smart-mouthed, smart-witted redhead with a big laugh and large appetites for fun, adventure, and other things. Not shy little scaredy cats who fainted at the sight of fire. That was the kind you took home to mama and she approved of. He liked the ones mama disliked on first sight, just to be contrary. But she had been a cutie, and he'd had to stifle the urge to take her in his arms and comfort her. He was not the comforting kind. He was more the aftercare kind, he reminded himself.

Parking at the store, he went in and grabbed some fried chicken and containers of slaw and potato salad. The nice thing about girls you brought home to mom was that they could generally cook. When he got the urge for a home cooked meal, he had to beg an invitation to someone's house or find a girl to take out to dinner and hope she'd cook breakfast the next morning. He could grill a mean steak and scramble eggs, knew how to make a country fried steak and mashed potatoes, but that was about the extent of it.

Getting home, he smiled at his little cabin on the lake. Nice and secluded. He'd heard there was a new bed and breakfast going up someplace around here, up north on the other side of the lake. Maybe he'd drive around sometime while he was off and look for it. Just to be nosy and to make sure it wasn't close enough where a bunch of tourists were going to bother his seclusion. On good weekends, sometimes he didn't see anyone for the entire four days he was off. Other times he did stupid things like volunteer to work.

He enjoyed the kids' firehouse though. It had been a donation from one of the people in town. They'd saved her house and she'd been grateful. It was fun to take it out and watch the kids learn fire safety and get to slide down the pole. He enjoyed it and it always made him want his own ankle biters. What would he do with one? He walked into his little cabin and looked around. It was perfect for him, but a wife and a kid? Yeah. He'd have to make adjustments to his well-managed life where he did what he wanted when he wanted.

He didn't do anything he didn't want, except laundry. No one liked to do laundry, but he lived how he liked. If he found someone, on the upside, he'd have someone to cook and do his laundry. He grinned and said out loud, "Yeah, that's how to get a wife. Threaten to give her chores." He imagined the little brunette would fold his shirts just the way he liked them. He wasn't going to think about anything else she might do, just the way he liked it done. He liked redheads.

Chapter 2

Beth walked into the kitchen Saturday morning, heart pounding. This was it. Her foray back into the real world. She poured her coffee and looked at her sister getting ready to leave. Joni would now commence to fuss, she knew. "I'm good, Joni, and yes, I really am," she said before Joni could start.

Joni shook her head as she rinsed her coffee cup and put it in the drainer.

"I'm glad you are getting out," she said, sounding as if she were picking her words. "This is going to be pretty busy with a lot of people though."

Beth nodded. "I know. I offered. Ellie didn't pressure me into it. It isn't like a jail cell. If I get, well, you know, I can just leave and come home."

"Yeah, that's true," Joni said. "And you promise you will keep in touch?"

"Joni, you are going to be on the same little patch of ground! It isn't like I'm going to be on the other side of the state or something. You can check on me. Who knows, we might even be working together. I don't know where Ellie is putting me."

Shaking her head, Joni said, "No, I'm working the pie throwing booth, it's all teachers and aides. Raising money for the junior high girls' softball uniforms and maybe some traveling expenses."

"You getting pied?" Beth asked. Hard to believe her pretty sister who always had her make up done would take a pie in the face.

Joni laughed. "No, I'm taking tickets and keeping the whipped cream pies ready. I wonder what you will be doing? Oh, don't forget your sunscreen. You know how easily you burn."

"I have it," Beth held up her little bag as she sipped her coffee. "I'll be home before supper. I told Ellie I had to knock off about five. I want to get back early. You know. You planning to be here?"

"Nah, I'll eat at the festival," she said. "I hear they are having fried candy bars and if that doesn't sound like a good supper, I don't know what is."

Despite her jangling nerves, Beth giggled. "Okay, I'll either see you later this evening or tomorrow morning then."

"Oh, I'm sure I'll see you there." Joni grabbed her bag. "I'm riding with Hank, he's got all the supplies in the truck, so you can have the car if you want."

Beth shook her head. "I'll just walk, but thanks." One thing she would have to do eventually was buy a car. She sold hers before they moved down here and hadn't felt the need for one since. If she ever needed one, she could borrow Joni's. Rarely feeling the need to leave though, she rarely did. However, if she planned to go out and about more, well, she'd just see how today went.

"Is that what you are wearing?" Joni asked. "It's supposed

to be in the 80's today — unseasonably warm. Won't you be hot?"

Beth looked down at her skinny jeans, sneakers and short sleeved cotton blouse in what she thought was a fun flower print. "I don't think so. I'm pretty sure I'll be fine."

Joni had on, she noted, a light yellow sundress and white sandals. She looked like the epitome of a sunbeam. She did feel a little under or casually dressed in her clothes, but knew she wouldn't be comfortable wearing less. Being a bit warm was a small price to pay for comfort. "Well, pack another shirt in your bag in case you sweat through that one," Joni told her, holding up her bag. "I have shorts and a tank top in here, plus a t-shirt. Who knows where Ellie is going to put you, but I know I'll be out in the sun all day."

"Sounds good," Beth said, making herself some peanut butter toast.

"And don't forget to call me if you need to," Joni fussed some more and Beth bit back a sigh of frustration.

"I promise and I will come home if I need to," Beth said. Joni meant well, and well, this was her first real foray out. Both of them were a little nervous. She flashed Joni what she thought was a reassuring smile and held out her hands. "See, not shaking or anything."

"Got water bottles? Keep hydrated," Joni started, but Beth shook her head.

"Aww, come on, Joni, you are going to freak me out if you keep this up."

"I'm sorry," Joni said, and gathered her things. "Okay, you are right and I'm out of here. Have a great time today and I will see you around later, I'm sure." Joni stopped at the door and looked at her. "Be careful, Bethie but I hope you have a really good time. You deserve one."

"Thanks, Joni," Beth said as she went to finish getting ready, ignoring as much as possible the flutters in her stomach.

Nerves, but she could be scared and still do it scared. Day one of getting back to the land of the living. She had this.

Fifteen minutes later, she headed out the front door into the warm May sunshine and toward the town square.

Walking down the neighborhood streets, she relaxed. She walked these streets most days. They had watched Lucy's little dogs, Juliet and Gypsy while she and Max were on their honeymoon. As much as she'd enjoyed walking them every day, she wasn't ready for the full time responsibility of a dog yet. Sure, one might make her feel safer, but she spent a lot of time locked in her little office. If today worked out though, and she was out a little more, who knew?

As she got closer to the center of town, the streets got a little narrower and the houses closer together, till they started turning into businesses. She remembered the town square from when she was a little kid. It had been thriving and they'd been down there often. Some of her best memories were walking downtown to the square with Joni, Sydney, and her grandma and grandpa. They would put her and her sisters in lawn chairs in the front row and then they would go sing with the town choir. She smiled, yes, there used to be a town choir which gave free concerts in the summer. Back in the good old days that Ellie was trying so hard to bring back. Would she join a choir if one were started? She hadn't sung since, well, she put that thought out of her mind and looked up at the gloriously clear blue sky. It was unseasonably warm for a May morning in southern Illinois and she rarely spent an entire day outside so planned to enjoy every minute of it.

Arriving at the town square, she crossed by Jordyn's bakery, Baking Memories, and began looking for Ellie. She said she'd be somewhere in the vicinity of the bandstand or amphitheater or whatever it was called, which sat on the north side of the square, so Beth headed that way. She saw the pie booth set up where Joni and Hank seemed to be bickering about something, so gave them a berth. If she couldn't find Ellie, she'd go ask Joni where she might be, but the square wasn't that big, and it wasn't seriously crowded yet. She'd find her.

There were food trucks parked along the side of the road, and she inhaled, already smelling the spicy beef cooking. Beef kabobs! That would be lunch later, she decided, then smiled. Sounded like she committed to staying till at least lunch.

She saw Ellie standing over in a corner of the bandstand with a few people around her, and walked over to wait her turn. Ellie seemed to know what she was doing, and sent the people on their way quickly. "Beth!" she said, when it was her turn.

"Ellie! Put me in, Coach!"

Ellie lowered her voice, and said, "Anytime you need anything or just want to go, you do it, okay?"

Ellie blushed, hating people knowing her issues, though she assumed Joni had shared a few details with friends. "Thank you, Ellie. Where will I be?"

"I figured you'd be comfortable working with kids?" Ellie asked, and Beth nodded. Sure. Kids were fun.

"Okay, great. You'll be helping Nick Kinkirk at the kids' firehouse. He's talking about fire safety and you can help the kids as they slide down the pole. That should be okay, right?"

Beth nodded, mind racing. Her blue-eyed fireman? How many firemen Nicks were there? It had to be him. Was she okay with that? Well, she sure didn't want to cause a scene and Ellie was already talking to the next group of volunteers. Heart racing, she walked over to the kids' court at the corner of the square, fenced in with a small temporary fence and several games were set up inside along with the firehouse. It brought memories of going to the fair with her grandparents back to her. There was a bounce house, and a knock down the bottles throwing game and several others that she remembered as a kid. Where was hot fireman though? Maybe he wouldn't remember her? It was basically her only hope of getting out of here with some dignity intact. He probably saw so many people in one day she blended in with the crowd. All she'd done since she moved here was try to blend in and she knew she'd succeeded for the most part. She never used to blend in, she stood out. People noticed her and she'd loved it. But that was in the past. Blending was good now.

Taking a deep breath, she smiled looking around and went to the little firehouse facsimile she finally spied on the edge of the kids' court. It was so cute, looking just like an old-fashioned firehouse with a statue of a Dalmatian out front, and a large sliding pole in the middle. The kids would climb up the side stairs and slide down. Part of her wished it was bigger. She wanted to slide down the pole! There was a huge stack of little plastic firefighter hats and a few boxes of bags that held giveaways, she assumed. But where was the hot fireguy?

"Hey, are you my helper?" There was his voice. Where was he? He came around the corner carrying another big box of stuff.

"I am," she said, ignoring that little leap her heart gave and demanding that her breathing remain stable. "I'm Beth."

"Hi, Beth, I'm Nick," he said. "Oh, yeah, I know you. You're the lawn fire the other day."

Beth couldn't help the giggle. "Is that how you classify people? By what caught on fire?"

"Yeah, and other things. Fire isn't the only thing we respond to. So, are you okay?"

Beth nodded. "I am and appreciate so much that—"

He cut her off with a wave of his hand. "How did you get roped into this?"

"My sister is a friend of Ellie's."

He nodded. "That will do it. Anyone she knows gets

pushed into service. Me, doing community service is part of the job and this is a fun little gig."

He showed her around the small house, explaining what all they did. "But anyway, all the kids care about is sliding down the pole and the plastic hat."

"Of course. They are kids," she said. "This should be fun!"

"Capacity is eight at a time, so your job is the door. Give them a hat, let them in a couple at a time, herd the parents to the side door to pick them up, and when you see those come out, send a few more in."

"I can handle that," Beth said. "Do I get a hat?"

"And a badge for the day," he said, reaching in the box and handing her a hat.

"This is heavy!" she said.

"You ought to feel the rest of the uniform," he said, and picked up a badge. He leaned over and efficiently pinned it on her shirt. "There you go."

Once again, she had to force her breath to remain steady. All that yoga was paying off. Her chest almost burned where his fingers had brushed against her. What was wrong with her? Years of being alone. Nothing more, she assured herself. Her body still worked. It was just her mind that had closed itself off.

"Porta johns are over there," he said. "If you need a break, just let me know. There will be lulls, then a rush, lulls then a rush. I don't know why, but that's how it works."

He had a bit of an accent, or a drawl, she noted, but couldn't really tell what kind. Southern? Maybe. She liked it whatever it was. It felt comforting and warm. Probably his professional tone. They probably taught that in first responder class. 'This is how you speak to upset people'. Yet, she wasn't upset and maybe he just remembered her as the grass fire and not the fainter. He probably ran into upset and fainting people all the time.

"I got it," she said. "I used to waitress in high school. I remember the lulls and the rushes. What time do we open?"

"In about half an hour," he said. "If you want to use the facilities or get a drink or something."

"I'm good," she said. "So have you done this long?"

"Worked the kids' firehouse? We were gifted it a couple years ago, so since we got it. I'm not the only one who does it, but it's my day off and the fishing will be there tomorrow."

"Avid fisherman? My granddad used to take us fishing out on the lake. It's great out there."

"Part of the reason I moved here was for the lake," he said. "Grew up a water rat."

Beth looked at him, startled. "I'm sorry?"

He laughed and she loved the way it sounded, clear and strong. "No, that's a good thing. Means I grew up on a boat, in the water, around the water."

"So you grew up to use water for work," she nodded, sagely, she hoped. "I get it."

"Coincidence," he said. "Granddad, Dad and Mom were all firefighters. It's in my blood, like the water."

"Sounds like you haven't moved far from your upbringing," she noted, watching him stack more hats.

"How about you? You lived here all your life?" He looked up at her and once again, her breath caught with the shock of his electric blue eyes.

Beth averted her eyes and shook her head. "No, we grew up near Chicago, but Joni and I moved down here a few years ago. We both needed a change and Grandma's house was empty, so there you go."

"Clearwater is a great town," he said. "There. I'm ready when they are."

"It is a great town," she agreed. "I've been very happy here."

"Have you?" he asked her, his eyes seeming to look inside her brain. She didn't like that feeling one little bit. "Here come the kids."

They settled into a very nice rhythm quickly and ushered dozens of kids through the firehouse, and when she looked across the square, she could see many bobbing red helmeted heads out there. Made her miss her natural hair color. Once again, she thought about letting it grow out. Was she ready? Well, she'd see how she felt tomorrow. This was the first day she'd spent hours out in a crowd, and away from the house. Sure, she'd gone to a few things with Joni, but never alone, and never for this long. Surprisingly, she was doing very well.

"You ready for some lunch?" Nick asked her a few hours later.

Beth shrugged. "Whenever."

He handed her a cardboard clock that said, 'Out to Lunch. Back at—' "It's just after 12:30," he said. "Set it for 2 and if we get back earlier, they will be thrilled. Makes people a lot less grumpy if they think they won't get something till 2 and you get it done by 1:30 than the other way around. Under promise and over achieve."

"Good customer service policy," she agreed as she set the clock and hung it on the hook on the door while he moved the boxes inside the house.

"Come on," he said. "I get paid to feed you lunch, so get whatever you want."

"You don't have to do that," she protested.

"Sure I do. Otherwise I'd get in trouble and no one wants to be in trouble, do they?"

Beth shook her head, hiding her smile. Trouble was what she used to love to get into. The thrill of getting away with something and then an even bigger thrill of being caught and trying to squirm out of it and often succeeding. She sort of missed those old days. Sometimes.

"After we eat," she suggested as they walked toward the food trucks, "if we have time, I want to go throw a pie at my sister's sometimes boyfriend."

"What?" he asked. "A pie?"

"Sure. It's part of the teacher's fundraising project. You put a teacher in a booth and throw a pie at their face. It's fun!"

"Maybe for the thrower," he said. "You like to pie throw, do you?"

"Yeah. I pitched for my softball team for years." She missed that, too. Man, getting out in public was just bringing back the memories.

He looked at her oddly. "You don't look like the pitcher type."

Beth giggled. "What is a pitcher type?"

"Oh, you know. Loud, serious and assertive and, well, you know." He took her arm to steer her across a maze of hoses and wires. Her heart skipped a little. She liked the feel of his hand on her arm. It had been too long. That was all. Nothing more.

"Huh. I'll have to remember that if I ever put a uniform on again. 'Loud and you know'. I got it!"

Nick laughed and she smiled. He had a nice laugh. "Want a pulled pork or what?"

"Kabobs," she said, promptly, pointing down a couple trucks. "They were making them as I was walking in this morning and I have been thinking about them ever since."

"Kabobs it is, then," he said.

After getting their food and a soda, they walked over to the fountain to sit on an empty bench and watch the water rise and fall, listening to the sound of the crowd and water splashing. "The fountain is so pretty," she said. "Very soothing."

"It was a gift from Mayor Lydia's grandparents," he told

her. "I know that because her granddad worked in the fire department and people were talking about it once."

"How did you get to be a fireman?" she asked. "I hear it's hard to get into. Lots of people apply."

He nodded. "My folks were both firefighters, like I said," he replied. "So I grew up thinking that's what everyone did. I was lucky, sometimes you do have to know someone to get in, no matter how good you are. Luckily, I either inherited the genes or am just good at, and I love it, and the hours."

"What hours do you work?" she asked him.

"I work four twelves on, and then have four days off," he said. "I am basically gone for four days. Twelve hour days mean you go home and sleep and go back to work. There's been quite a few times when we've worked over that and I just stay there."

"I bet your wife misses you when you are gone," she said.

He nodded and she felt a strong smack of regret hit her. Of course he was married. He was too gorgeous not to be, and seemed like a nice guy on top of it. "Well, my boat misses me, and that's as close to a wife as I have," he said, taking her kabob container to throw away. "How about you? What do you do?" Okay, not married or at least not married anymore.

"Play on the computer," she said. It was her go to answer. "I actually work in claims for an insurance company. I try not to tell people that though, because then they hate me."

"I get that," he said. "We've all had to fight with insurance companies."

"Yeah, and we always 'win', right?" she air quoted. "That's what people think anyway."

"Do you like it?"

Beth shrugged. "I like the hours and the fact I can work at home." Her passion was graphic design, but other than a few little projects here and there she rarely did that any more. She glanced across the square to Jordyn's sign over her shop. It was gorgeous, she had to admit. Her design just popped with color and life.

"Homebody, are you?" he asked. "Let's see if we can find this booth of your sister's sometimes boyfriend."

"It's over there," she said. It was funny, she thought. Here she'd been worried about how she'd be today, but somehow felt normal. This must be how other people felt when they went out. It was hard to remember how she used to love the spotlight, and being stared at as she walked by. She hid her face now behind huge sunglasses and her mousy brown hair, and conservative clothes, but in the past... well, the past was the past. It had nothing to do with enjoying today, she reminded herself. And that was all she was doing. Enjoying the day. The gorgeous hunk of fireman was just a perk.

"Hey, Joni," she said. "You remember Nick?"

Joni gave him a look and Nick could almost feel himself shrivel. What?

"He's who Ellie assigned me to work with. We just had a lunch break and I want to pie Hank." Nick watched Joni almost seem to relax.

"Hi, Nick," she said, but coolly, as she turned to her sister. "What are you doing?"

"Working at the kids' block with the little kids fire station. I watch them slide down a pole. You know, important work. Here's my donation." She slipped some money in a jar. "Now let me throw a pie."

"You sure you want to?" Joni asked and Nick became even more intrigued What was the sister dynamic here? "I mean, he really needs pied, so far he's only gotten it a couple of times."

"Aww, little Beth can't throw that far," the man he assumed was Hank stuck his head out of the hole. "Let her try, Joni. It will be cute."

Joni and Beth looked at each other and giggled. Nick smiled at the sound. Then stepped back as Beth stretched and picked up a pie. Within seconds Hank was covered in whipped cream while she picked up another one. The girl had fine form, he thought. He still couldn't quite picture her up on the mound, but maybe so. In quick order, Hank had two more pies in his face while Joni laughed and Beth had a self-satisfied little smile on her face. He liked that. He could see a little spunk in her after all. So what was with the fainting the other day? He usually enjoyed the 'what you see is what you get' type, but this one? She intrigued him. Like a little present where you peeled back the layers.

"Want to throw one?" Joni asked him as she handed Beth a wipe.

Nick shook his head. "No way am I following that," he said. "Besides, we need to get back."

"See you this evening, Joni," Beth said.

"You doing okay?" he heard Joni all but whisper.

"I am," Beth whispered back, then said in a normal tone. "Bye, Hank. Hope you get many more pies!"

"Thanks, kiddo," he said. "Appreciate the sentiment."

They headed back to the kids' block and he waved at Ellie who was surrounded by people, holding her clipboard as usual. That little bit of a thing was a powerhouse, and more his type than this mousy little thing with the good pitching arm. But there was something about her. He didn't know what. He didn't have to, he told himself. It was just a day thing. They'd work a few hours together and that would be that.

They got back and he took the clock off the door and put it up. "Thank you for lunch," she said.

"You are welcome," he said. "It was good to have company. You'd be surprised how often I have to run this alone because the volunteer doesn't show up."

"That's not good," she frowned. "If you say you are going to do something, you should."

"Yeah, when I first started I wanted to track them down," he picked up a box of hats and moved it back where it was handy, "spank their bottoms and make them stand in a corner, but after a while, I just assumed they weren't showing. Once in a while, though, I'm quite pleasantly surprised."

He looked over at her and hid a grin. Yup, while he hadn't expected her reaction, she gave it to him. Maybe little miss mouse wasn't as delicate as she appeared.

There were kids already hanging around, waiting for them to reopen, so they started into what was already an easy rhythm. Beth didn't say much, he noticed, but had an easy way with the kids and their folks. He enjoyed her quiet presence as opposed to the louder more feisty women he was used to being with. He'd probably be bored in a matter of days, but for now, she felt like a calming presence, like going out fishing felt. He never got bored with that. What was he even thinking? He'd probably never see her again and she could have a boyfriend for all he knew. Heck, she could be married with six kids. Nah, she would have mentioned that, he felt sure.

He looked across the crowd as a spot of bright red hair caught his eye. He casually watched it bob and weave through the crowd until she landed next to Beth. Gorgeous little thing, he thought, too young for him, but a cutie, nonetheless. He frowned. Didn't he know her?

"Hey, Moriah," he heard Beth say. "Jordyn let you out for the day?"

Redhead shook her head. "Just on a quick break. I was looking for Lucy, have you seen her?"

"No, need me to send her to the bakery if I do, though?"

"Yeah, I needed to tell her something. Sister stuff. Better get back to baking the cupcakes. See you, Beth." Oh, that was where he'd seen her. Working at the bakery where he bought coffee and donuts quite often. Pretty little thing, feisty and fairly talented in the kitchen for someone so young. He wasn't interested in dating someone who was barely twenty if that, but she was more his type than the mouse.

Nick shook his head as he got back to work. Two more hours, then he was heading to the lake. He always thought best at the lake. What did he even have to think about? Maybe that was what he had to think about.

At the end of the day, Beth helped him pack up his truck which she noticed was much cleaner than Joni's car. "Some of the guys are coming over this evening to haul the house away," he told her. "So we are all done. I really appreciated your help today. Made the time fly."

"I had a good time," she told him. "Thanks for making it so enjoyable."

"You're welcome," he said. "Oh, do you need me to sign a paper?"

She cocked her head at him, looking puzzled. "I don't think so?"

"Some people need evidence of volunteer hours for an employer or school credit or something," he explained.

Beth ran her fingers through her thick hair, and he swore he saw some red highlights in there. "Nope. I'm just here out of the goodness of my heart today," she said. "Well, thanks, Nick. See you around."

He felt a little reluctant to let her go, but wasn't sure why and couldn't think of a reason to keep her. "Bye, Beth, good to work with you. See you." She gave him a little wave and took off down the street while he watched her walk away. Then heard his phone buzz the firehouse ring, and sighed while he answered it. There went his fishing time, he imagined.

Beth walked back into the house not long after. Joni was already there, she could tell, which was weird because she said she was staying into the evening. "Beth?" She heard an odd note in Joni's voice.

"Who else?" Walking into the kitchen, she saw Joni staring out the back window at the garden, before she turned around. "You okay? You and Hank have a fight again?"

"No. Well, maybe, actually, we just ran out of pies and closed early, but Bethie, did you leave the back door unlocked? When you left this morning?"

Beth stared at her and said emphatically, "I did not. Why? Was it unlocked?"

Joni nodded. "I came in the back way from Hank's after we got done, and it was unlocked."

Beth looked around wildly. "Is someone here?"

Joni shook her head. "No. I had Hank come over and we searched the house, no one under the beds or in the closets."

Beth's mouth felt dry. "Root cellar? Attic?"

"All clear. And nothing was moved as far as I could tell. But I knew you wouldn't leave the back door unlocked."

Beth felt as if she would break if she moved. "You're sure no one is in here?"

Joni rushed over and hugged her. "I'm sure, but if you want, we can go to a hotel tonight, or over to Hank's to stay."

Beth thought, then said slowly, "Nope. Not letting anyone run me anywhere again. I probably did leave it unlocked. I was a little nervous this morning, you know and might not have thought about it." Joni threw her a look that meant she didn't believe it. Beth didn't really believe it either, but what else could it be? That had to be it. There was no other thing. "Don't we have the video from the camera?" she asked.

Joni sighed. "Nope, nothing. I'm not sure it's working right."

"We need to get it looked at," Beth said. "Call the people and have them come out and make sure everything is working right."

"Okay, we will do that tomorrow. You sure you don't want to go somewhere tonight?" she asked.

"Yeah, I'm sure," she said. "Though if you wanted your boyfriend to stay over, that would be okay."

Joni laughed. "Well, that's a turn around. I guess that makes him part of the family, huh?"

"Not till he puts a ring on it," Beth retorted, but with a forced smile. Was she okay? She wasn't certain. She'd do her own inspecting and checking before bed, Just for her own peace of mind. Surely it wasn't starting again. It couldn't. Things had been peaceful for over two years now. They hadn't had any issues since they moved here. There was no way that things, no. Just no. Especially since today had been the first day, she had spent as a normal person in ages. Right when she was thinking she was safe again. Beth straightened her shoulders. She was safe. This meant nothing, and it was a coincidence and nothing more. No way was she going back to hiding when she'd taken the first step. It simply wasn't happening. The girl she used to be was still in there somewhere, and she was bound and determined to let her out again. Her life had been on hold for too long.

"Okay," Joni said. "I'll call Hank and maybe he can grill out for us. I'm still a little afraid of that new fancy grill he made me get. Did you eat today?"

Beth nodded. "I did. Nick and I had kabobs for lunch."

"He seems like a really nice guy," Joni said.

"He does," Beth agreed with her but thought, not her type. What was her type? Strong, determined, masterful and domineering? A guy who loved to tame a brat? Yeah, look where that got her. Had her landing here in Clearwater a long way from her softball team and her office that she'd loved so much. Hard to believe she was still that person who couldn't wait to go to work every day in an office full of people. Where she'd been the life of the party, the lead singer at karaoke, and the star of the softball team. Attracted all the attention at the bars where she and a group of friends who weren't Joni's hung out.

She half smiled as she turned to go to her room. Her ball team would be appalled at what she turned into, and her office coworkers would never believe she had three locks on her office door. She'd always had an open door policy and thrived on the noise and chaos and did her best work in the midst of it.

And one person had changed all that.

Well, really, she was the one who changed. Was it self-preservation or had she just tucked her tail between her legs and run away? Some days she knew it was the former, and other days she suspected it was the latter. One thing she knew for sure was she would always be grateful to Joni for helping her get out. One unlocked door in three years meant nothing, and tomorrow they would get all the locks double checked but probably tonight she would lock herself in the office and work all night. No way would she be able to sleep. Joni would have Hank, but she knew she'd just lie in bed staring at the ceiling and freaking out over every noise the old house would make. Usually those were comforting noises, but tonight, well, she knew better.

Beth looked in the fridge to see if there were any leftover side dishes in there or if she needed to make something while Joni ran over to talk to Hank. Nothing that excited her so she started water boiling for mac and cheese and opened a can of kidney beans to begin making three bean salad. That should be plenty. She wasn't really hungry, but would need fortification for the long night ahead.

Opening the fridge again to grab some milk, butter and cheese for the macaroni, her eye fell on the door. She felt her ears buzz and her vision started to go black. No. Just no.

Taking a deep breath, then another one, she picked up the

small jar of almond stuffed olives – which she knew for a fact could not be bought in Clearwater – and took them to the trash can. Then she closed the trash bag and took it outside to the curb while ignoring the buzzing in her ears and the fading in and out vision. Grappling with the idea, the concept, the knowledge that, now, okay, he was here. He'd been in their house. He'd brought her the stuffed olives he knew she loved, and left them in the refrigerator. Any doubt she'd had, vanished. Why? What did he want? Surely it wasn't a kiss and make up present. Biting back a hysterical giggle, she shuddered hard.

Now what? Though she went back in and finished the sides, she knew she wasn't going to be able to eat. Her head felt as if it were off in never-never land. Just floating. At least her ears weren't buzzing anymore like they had the other day when she'd fainted or whatever it was she'd done.

She looked over at Joni when she walked in. "Hank is manning the grill," she said. "You okay?"

Beth nodded. "I just got a call from work," she said through a dry mouth, making it up on the fly. "I'm going to have to work all night. I tell you what, I'll be locked in my office from nine to about 6 in the morning, so why don't you and Hank spend the night at his house?"

Joni shook her head. "I'm not leaving you alone."

"Joni, I'll be locked in my office with my alarms set and not coming out all night. I'll feel better if you are over at Hank's, you know? I know I'll be safe."

"I'll think about it," Joni conceded. "What's burning?"

"The mac and cheese," Beth pulled it off the burner and felt a little weirded out by the normalcy of cooking. Her life had just been turned upside down and she didn't want to deal with it right now. She'd tell Joni in the morning. Tonight, she just couldn't. As long as she knew Joni was safe and she would be at Hank's house, then she would be safe in her little office/safe room. She would bury herself in work, and then a few games and pass the night. She'd napped in her chair before and could again, but doubted she'd be settled enough to do that. Who knew though?

———

"Hi, Robyn," Beth heard Joni say the next morning. "Come on in. I don't know what all you need to look at or see. Let me tell my sister you are here."

Beth unlocked the office door and yelled out, "I'll be there in a minute, quick bathroom break!" She sighed, relieved that the alarm company remembered her special request for only female techs. Robyn had been there once before for their semi-annual alarm check-up. She knew what she was doing.

Finishing up in the bathroom, she headed to the living room. Robyn, a tall, blonde, capable woman said, "So why am I here? What happened? I was just here a couple months ago and everything was working fine."

Beth opened her mouth, but Joni said, "We got home yesterday and the back door was unlocked. We never leave it unlocked. Nothing showed up on the camera though. Something has to be wrong."

Beth started to say she probably left it unlocked but shut her mouth. She hadn't and she knew it. In any case, it was not going to hurt to have everything checked.

Robyn nodded as she took a couple notes on her tablet. "Okay, part of our new program is that if I come for a call for any reason, I have to call someone to check the fire and carbon monoxide alarms at the same time. Beth, I don't know who it is but they are sending someone out. Are you okay with it?"

Beth nodded. "I'm okay," she said, wondering how Robyn knew it was her and not Joni, but decided not to ask. Was she that easy to read despite her many desperate ways she'd tried to disguise herself and blend into the woodwork?

"Okay, then they will be here soon, and I'm going to get to work." Robyn stood up and Beth nodded again. She was beginning to feel like a bobble head.

The doorbell rang and Joni went to answer it. Beth peeked over at the door, holding her breath. There at the door, stood Nick in all his uniformed glory.

Chapter 3

"Hi, you're Nick, right?" she heard Joni say and Beth felt a rush of relief. Why? That he wasn't anyone else? Of course. "Come on in."

Swallowing hard, Beth straightened her back and looked up at him. "I thought you were on the lake today," she said as if she knew everything and wasn't concerned about anything. Why? Why was she pretending. Part of who she was, she guessed. Her new her, anyway.

He grinned at her and, again, she just felt better. Safer. Why? Obviously, that was a question with no answer. "Best laid plans, you know. Someone had a death in the family and I'm filling in."

"I'm sorry," she said.

"Hi, Nick, I'm Robyn, here from the alarm company. You know what you are doing, I assume?" Beth did not like the way Robyn looked at him which was absolutely ridiculous. He was not a piece of meat to drool over! He was here to do a job!

"Checking alarms," he told her. "Beth, I want to start

upstairs and work my way down. Want to show me where they are?"

"Oh, that's okay," Joni said. "I can do that."

Nick shook his head. "Robyn needs you to help her with the door and window alarms," he said and Beth bit her lip so she wouldn't smile. He just took charge of that situation, didn't he? "Come on, Beth," he said as if she were just going to stand up and go upstairs alone with him. Which, for some reason, she was going to do. His authoritarian attitude didn't seem overbearing or bullying, though, just calm and like he knew what he was doing. Of course, he did. It was his job. Her brain raced around and around like a hamster on a never ending wheel.

She stood up and smiled at Joni. "I'm okay with Nick," she said. "We worked together all day yesterday, after all."

"You're sure?" Joni asked. At her nod, she said, "Okay, Robyn, I'm all yours. Let's get the other alarms checked out."

Beth led Nick up the stairs toward the bedrooms. "Nice house," he said, calmly, then as she pointed out the first alarm, said, "so, Beth. Why am I here today? I checked the records. The alarm company did this check just three months ago when it was scheduled."

Beth ached to tell him. Never in her life had she wanted to spill her guts and the entire story – the entire story no one but Joni really knew – so badly. She didn't know him though. Sure, they'd spent yesterday together, and he seemed nice, but what did she know about him? Not much.

"Spill it, Beth. You don't want to find yourself over my knee, do you?"

For some reason, that made her giggle. Well, almost giggle. "Think I'm teasing, do you?" he said, almost playfully while taking something from his pocket.

She nodded, but said, "When we got home yesterday, the

back door was unlocked and nothing showed up on the camera. But–"

"But, what?" he asked, taking the cover off the alarm.

"I just know someone was in here."

"How do you know?" he asked, and they moved on to the next alarm.

"I just do," she said.

"Someone you know, you think?" he asked casually.

She wanted to tell him. So badly. But she couldn't. No one could know. Instead, she just shrugged. "We just want to be safe," she said, watching him replace the next alarm cover.

"Clearwater is a safe little town," he said as they headed down to the main floor. "Have you had any trouble?"

He wasn't a cop, she reminded herself. He was a fire-fighter. If she told anyone, it should be a cop, not some random guy who seemed nice enough. Besides, it was the truth. "No, we've been very safe and comfortable here," she said. Until now.

She heard Joni's cell go off in the next room as Nick pulled out the step ladder they had put in the corner earlier. "Mom? What's wrong, Mom? Are you okay? Something wrong with Sydney? Beth? No, Beth's okay. She's right here. Mom, what's going on?" There was a pause as Beth listened, her heart racing. "Here she is. You can talk to her yourself. Mom, she's fine. She's not even left the house today." She walked in and handed her phone to Beth. "Mom thinks you've been in an accident."

Beth took the phone, and noticed her hands were trembling. "Mom, it's me. Beth. I'm fine. I'm right here with Joni. What's going on?" Their mom, usually cool and calm as a capable surgeon should be, sounded almost hysterical.

"Beth? Is it you? Is it really?"

"Mom, yes. What's wrong? Take a breath. Talk to me."

She noticed Nick had perched on top of the ladder and was watching her.

"I had a phone call from the state police. They said you'd been in a car accident and weren't expected to make it. I already left work and called Joni and—"

"Mom! It had to be a mistake. I'm right here. I'm safe. I haven't driven anywhere in days."

"It wasn't a mistake," her mom insisted. "They described you and everything. Bethie, what's going on? Are you safe?"

Beth winced. Of course, their mom knew most of it. "Mom, I'm safe. I'm fine."

"What's our safeword, can you say it?"

What? Oh, yeah, the code they used when someone else had to pick them up from school, a friend's parent, or a taxi driver unexpectedly when she had to work late. "Rainbows and unicorns, Mom. I'm really safe."

Her tone changed to briskly professional. "I'm coming down anyway. I'll let you know when my flight lands."

"Okay, Mom," she said, and hung up, handing Joni back her phone. "Mom's on her way."

"Well, that will be fun," Joni said. "So what happened?"

Beth felt everyone's eyes on her. Heat rushed to her cheeks. Why did there have to be an audience? "I guess someone called her and said I'd been in an accident."

"Why would someone do that?" Robyn asked. "Not that it's any of my business."

Beth shrugged. "I don't know." She knew why and when her eyes rose to meet Nick's, she could tell he knew she was lying. Her fingernails bit into her palm so hard she thought she'd broken skin.

"Let's get these alarms checked," he said. "Back to work."

Joni and Robyn turned and went back to the porch door. "Soon as we are done here," he said, moving the ladder, "we're going out."

Beth shook her head. What did *out* mean? Away from here? She didn't want to leave Joni.

"Yes, so make whatever arrangements you need. Got another one of these in the basement?" She nodded but just stared at him. Why did he think he had any authority over her? He couldn't demand she go with him. Could he? She'd only met him yesterday, if you didn't count the time he came to the house before. Nick Kinkirk was not the boss of her.

Half an hour later, after making sure Joni was off with Hank, she found herself in the front seat of his truck. It had happened and she had been there while it happened, but she wasn't really sure how it happened.

"Where are we going?" she asked him, finally. "And why?"

"Out. I need some answers."

"Why? I'm nothing to you. We just met yesterday."

"Well, apparently, I'm involved now," he said, almost grimly.

"You don't have to be," she said. For some reason, she felt safe with him. And right, as if she'd known him forever. She'd never felt that way with—her brain shut it down. No way was she summoning the devil with her thoughts. Or her words. She looked at him wondering what he was thinking, and why.

"Yet, here I am." He seemed to be driving toward the lake.

"Where are we going?" she asked, looking around, wondering why she wasn't freaking out at basically being kidnapped. Part of her out of body experience. Like her brain wasn't even there. This actually wasn't a bad place to be. She could handle this. Plus, basically she hadn't slept last night or eaten since lunch yesterday, though she poked at her food so Joni wouldn't realize.

"My place," he said. "We need to talk."

"No. No. I don't want to go to your place!" What was he thinking!

"Why not? I cleaned up some." He said it like that mattered.

"I don't know you! What are you doing?"

"Rescuing a damsel?" he asked, and just kept driving.

"I am not a damsel," she snapped. Weirdly, just standing up for herself made her feel more like old Beth than she had in a few years. She was not a damsel in need of rescue. She could rescue her own darn self. Or hide in a castle like a Princess did, of course. Either way.

"Well, Damsel, apparently something happened and you don't want to talk about it in front of your sister. So we are going to my house so you can talk about it in front of me."

Beth opened her mouth to protest that Joni knew everything. Then decided not to bring what her sister knew or didn't into it. It didn't matter. "What business is it of yours? Why are you doing this?"

"No clue, Damsel. I just know it is."

"Don't you have to be at work?" she asked.

"I called in a favor."

"Why?" She felt beyond frustrated. "I don't know what is going on here. You don't even know me."

"Weird, isn't it?" he said, turning off the highway onto a gravel road lined with trees.

"Do you live in the seven dwarfs house in the middle of the woods?" she asked him, looking around. She hadn't been out this way since she was a kid. Why not? It was gorgeous out here. Right now, the trees were green and lush, full of color and life. Looking for the button, she rolled her window down. Yeah, she remembered that smell. The lake. Something about the smell of water. Forgetting for a minute why she was there and who she was with, she inhaled deeply and smiled.

Nick didn't say anything, but she felt his eyes on her and tension filled her again. For the first time in his presence, she felt uneasy. No one knew she was here. Joni wasn't expecting her back for hours.

"Take me home," she demanded.

"Almost there," he said in a tone that she assumed he meant to be reassuring, as he turned off the gravel road onto a smaller one lane road. "See?"

She tried not to gasp. It was utterly picture perfect. A little wooden log cabin with a huge front porch, wood stacked on one end, a couple of old rocking chairs settled cozily at the other end. The door was a dark forest green that blended with the forest surrounding it. "It's gorgeous," she told him. "But I don't want to go in. I want to go home."

"Yet, you are going in," he said, parking the truck. She folded her arms and stared straight ahead as he walked around the truck and opened the door. Then reached over her and unbuckled her seatbelt. He smelled vaguely like fire and smoke, probably from his uniform. It wasn't an unpleasant smell at all. "Come on. Don't make me carry you. I'm a fireman. You can go over my shoulder as fast as you can go over my knee."

Sighing, Beth moved her feet and turned, almost bumping into him as he stood too close to the door. "I'm walking," she informed him. "And you need to stop threatening to spank me. It's not very gentlemanly."

"Never claimed to be a gentleman, and really, it wouldn't be any bother at all to spank some sense into you or the truth out of you."

Beth rolled her eyes. The tension was still there, but the anxiousness had disappeared. She felt no fear out here, alone with him, despite his constant threats to put her over his knee. Fear, tension, and nerves had been her companion for the last few years. So what was wrong with her that the circumstances had ramped up and yet, she was almost eerily calm? No sleep last night and no food today? Yeah, that probably contributed. His fireman presence? Maybe that too.

They walked into the small cabin and she smiled at the bookshelf lining one wall, the small kitchen tucked under a window overlooking the woods, and a very cozy sofa in front of a wood burning fire place. It really needed prettied up a little, what her mother would call a woman's touch, but it was comfortable and comforting. She frowned, though, thinking of her mother.

"You don't like it?" he asked, going over and opening a curtain so sunlight streamed in.

"I love it," she confessed. "I was just thinking about my mom coming in."

"Have a seat," he pointed to the couch. "I'll make us a drink."

She sat and looked around. Two doors, she assumed one was the bathroom, and the other the bedroom. It was a sweet little bachelor pad. A minute later, he came over, and handed her what she sipped and found out was root beer. It was nice he hadn't even asked what she wanted, but she didn't know why. She felt cared for.

"So," he said, settling down next to her. "Where should we begin? What's your deal with fire?"

"Fire?" She looked at him, quizzically. "I don't have a thing about fire?"

"Why did you have a panic attack and pass out when your sister caught the grass on fire, then?"

Beth put her drink down on the coaster on the wooden coffee table and shook her head. Was she telling him this? Probably. "It wasn't the fire." She could hear Joni scream in her head. *"Beth! Call 911, someone call 911!"* That had been the last thing she'd remembered for a few days back then.

"Then?" he prompted. "Beth, you are stuck here till I

drive you back. I'm not doing that till I know what's going on."

"What if it isn't your business?" She glared at him and it irritated her that he smiled.

"It wasn't my business before, but it seems to be now. I'm involved. How, why? I don't know. I just know I am. So spill, Damsel, tell me all."

"You coulda put something harder in that drink if you wanted to hear all my dirty secrets," she grumbled.

"Dirty?" he said, raising his dark eyebrows. Why did it feel like she had always known him? "Well, this should be good."

Beth rolled her eyes, once again, feeling more 'her' than she had felt in a long time. Why? Why wasn't she terrified? Or pissed or something, instead of just vaguely annoyed, and yes, even a little turned on. It wasn't like this was a date or anything.

"It wasn't the fire," she started. "It was Joni."

"Go on," he said.

Beth sighed. "It was like a flashback. The last time I heard her yelling call 911."

"When was that time?" he asked her.

"Before we moved. She found me, well, on the floor in my apartment and I heard her scream my name and yelling for someone to call."

There. That should satisfy him. How did she already know it wouldn't?

"So what happened to you?" He wasn't going to give up, was he?

"Short story, I was attacked."

He nodded and put his glass on the table, too. "And the person, I assume, was never caught so you and your sister moved down here."

She shook her head. "He was caught, I knew who he was and where he worked, but he was released on a legal technicality. Then he started harassing me. Then we moved down here. Now–" She looked up at him. "Now, I think he's back."

"The unlocked back door?" he guessed.

She nodded.

"Lots of people make a mistake and leave a house unlocked," he said. "Doesn't mean anything."

"Joni and I, we never ever leave the house unlocked."

"And you are perfect and never mess up?"

"Yup. Exactly. Plus the fact," she hesitated. No. She wasn't telling him that. "There was nothing on the video camera, and I'm pretty sure he was in the house." There, that was close enough to the truth.

"Why do you think that?" he asked.

Shrugging, she said, "Just a feeling."

He folded his arms. "I don't think so."

She didn't say anything and he sighed. "So how dangerous is he?"

She shrugged again. "You'd think he'd be over it by now. It's been years."

"Why was he harassing you, do you know?"

Oh, yeah. She knew all right. Was she telling him? Oh, hell to the no! "Why does anybody do anything?" Well, that was weak.

"Beth, I mean what I say. I need to know what's going on and if I have to paddle it out of you, I will."

Beth couldn't help it. She snorted. "Sure. That's what will happen."

"Fine."

He took hold of her arm and tugged her closer, then grabbed her shoulder as she started to struggle. "What do you think you are doing?"

"I explained it to you," he said as he positioned her over his lap as if she weren't trying to get back up and was some sort of blow up doll he could do whatever he wanted to.

"Let me up!" She pounded on his leg and the couch as she twisted and tried to squirm off him. "What are you doing?"

"Finding out the truth," he said, and smacked her bottom while she kicked and wiggled.

"Stop it!" she demanded.

"Not till you are ready to confess," he said and started spanking her. He actually was following through on what he said and spanking her. Who did that? Nick Kinkirk apparently.

Her brain could barely comprehend what was happening. Her entire life suddenly was a series of weird, strange stuff. "Ow! Stop it!" She kicked harder and moved her hand back to try and block his hand while continuing to fight her way off him.

"Stop it!" she said. "That hurts!"

"Spankings hurt," he told her and didn't stop. "That's the point."

"Stop it. Ow!" She already felt worn out from struggling against this unmovable object with the very hard hand. "Stop it!"

He had her wrist held in his hand, holding it in the middle of her back and she felt utterly helpless and had a loss of control she didn't like at all.

"Nick! *Ow!* I mean it!" Her bottom hurt and the frustration was building. She would not give him the satisfaction of crying though. "No! Please!"

Okay, that one snuck out but she was feeling desperate, and exhausted. How could she make him stop? "Please, no more! It hurts! I'm sorry!" What was she sorry for? She didn't know. "Please, ow ow! I can't! Don't!"

Then out choked a huge sob that she tried her hardest to fight back. She would not cry. And yet she was. She'd never been spanked before, like this anyway, ever and she didn't like it one bit! "Stop it!" she screeched and this time the sob wouldn't be contained as he continued smacking her harder and harder till she thought she'd succumb to the pain. "No!"

Then she started sobbing. It was from frustration and lack of control plus the pain, it just hurt and there was nothing she could do about it. She hated this! Hated it. "Stop, just stop," she managed to say through her tears and sobs. "Please, please." He smacked her once more, harder and it made her howl. She'd never be able to sit again, ever. Why was he doing this to her? How could she make it stop? "Nick! Please! No more, I'll tell!" She thought that was what she said, but it sounded rather incoherent to her ears.

He finally relaxed his grip on her enough so she could slide off onto the floor onto her knees, where she buried her face in the couch and cried. How dare he do this to her? What did she feel more, pain, mortified or pissed off? She wasn't sure.

"Beth, are you ready to talk? Or do you need some more?"

"No more," she sobbed. "No more."

"Then sit up here like a big girl and talk to me," he said. Stubbornly, she shook her head. Last thing she wanted to do was look at him. "At three you'll be dropping those pants and going over for more," he warned. "One, two,"

Without thinking, she scrambled up and sat on the couch, wiping her tears with the back of her hand. He reached over and pulled out a few tissues, wiped her cheeks and then handed her another one. "Good choice, now blow your nose."

She wanted to say no again, but felt too defeated and too worn out to do anything but blow her nose. My, how the mighty had fallen, she told herself. She'd needed one of those five or six years ago and maybe things that happened, well... He took the tissue from her and tossed it.

"I didn't like that," she told him, still unable to look him in the eye.

"That was the point, yet you took it."

Like she had a choice.

"So, are you ready to talk to me now?" he asked, then put his arm around her, and pulled her into a hug. "You are safe with me," he told her. "Just let me help, Damsel. I can help."

She shook her head but let him put his arm around her and snuggle her close to him. Why did she want to climb on his lap and sob? She didn't, she wanted to stop crying and he was the one who humiliated and spanked her. He was no comfort. Yet. he seemed to be. Why? What was it with him?

"So how did it start?" he asked.

"I ruined his life." There. She said it. Apparently it wasn't the words he expected because she felt him react. Maybe he'd let her go home now, and realize she didn't deserve to be helped. Because she didn't. Beth choked on a sob again and realized he was waiting.

"I didn't used to be this way," she said, touching her hair and modest clothes. "I used to be hot stuff."

"Hot stuff, huh?" He said it as if he didn't really believe her. That was rather insulting.

"Yeah, my natural hair color is a dark red, and it was almost to my waist." She felt him start again with that one. "I had the attitude to go with the hair. I was valedictorian of my high school class, graduated with honors from college, got a hot shot job as a graphic designer and earned one promotion after another. On weekends, I was the star pitcher on the softball team and had a big circle of friends. I thought I was, as my grandma said, 'all that and a bag of chips', whatever that means."

She paused to let all that sink in, to him, and to her. That person seemed another lifetime ago. Another person ago, one whom she couldn't even imagine now. How could she be so young and innocent, headstrong and self-assured? It truly didn't seem real.

"Say something," she finally said when he remained quiet. It was his fault, he was the one who wanted to know, after all.

She would have been just fine with a not sore butt if he hadn't insisted on a confession in his own so very charming way.

"I wasn't expecting this," he said.

"Well, it gets worse," she assured him. "You want to take me home now?

"Nah, I'm a sucker for a mystery. Keep going, Damsel."

She frowned at what she felt fairly certain would be her new nickname if she ever saw him again after today, and that was doubtful. However, he pulled her close again, which for some reason made her feel not only comforted but willing to tell the entire sordid story. Last time she told it, she'd been alone in a room with a judge and two lawyers who were telling her the case wasn't going to happen, he wouldn't be tried.

"So anyway, one night about ten of us were out bar hopping, and this guy came up and asked me to dance. I blew him off, I wasn't in the mood to dance, I wanted to be with my friends. So at the next two bars we went to, there he was again, and I finally said yes the third time." She shrugged. "We were together that night and for the next month or so. I thought it was love."

"Instant attraction," he said. "Keep going."

"He did all the right things, flowers, candy, presents, jewelry, a couple weekends away. He found out I'm crazy about these expensive almond stuffed olives and made sure I had a jar in the refrigerator all the time. I was young and swept away. Then one day, I was out to lunch and saw him and another woman. I didn't think a lot about it because I often had lunch with people from work but I got back and I guess it did bother me a little because I started to do some digging. I'm good on the computer."

"Married?" Nick asked.

"Married, had a kid and worked for his father-in-law as did his wife. I let the anger and hurt build up for a few days and took my self-righteous self over to his office mid-morning when a lot of people would be there. I dumped all the presents he'd gotten me on his wife's desk along with movie ticket stubs, hotel stationery, all that kind of stuff. Announced as loudly as I could what he'd done to me and swept out like I was a Queen."

"Bet that didn't go over well," Nick said. She couldn't tell if he was appalled or what. She was. She couldn't imagine doing anything like that now.

"Yeah, like I said. I ruined his life. His wife left him, his father-in-law fired him, they wouldn't let him see his kid, his lawyers bankrupted him and then he decided to, well, stalk and harass me. It started slow, but kept ramping up despite a protection order, and one night he came over and, well, Joni found me the next day and I was in the hospital for three days."

Beth felt him stiffen but kept talking. "He was arrested before I got out, but before the trial something paperworky happened. They said legally they couldn't prosecute him, he was free and I was terrified."

"So you moved down here," he said.

"Yeah, Joni wouldn't let me come alone and our sister Sydney came down for a while. Mom wanted to come, but she's too enmeshed in the hospital up in Chicago. Clearwater just doesn't have all the fancy gadgets she loves in the oper-ating room."

"That... I can't even imagine that. An entire family uprooted and running."

Beth nodded. "Because of me."

"Because of him," Nick corrected her as she squirmed on her still hot bottom.

"My actions caused his reaction, just like his actions caused mine," she said. "I'm not innocent in this."

"And now, a few years later, he's back?"

Beth nodded. "I know he is."

"How do you know?"

"I just do," she said. "He found me and I don't know what he wants."

"But you suspect?"

Beth nodded. "To hurt me, or ruin my life like I did his. You know what's funny?"

"What is funny?" he asked and stroked her arm. "I need some funny."

"The other day when I went out to the square to work with you was the first day, well, I decided I was going to rejoin the world. I'd had enough hiding, enough not having any friends, enough of the four walls of my office. And now."

"And now," he echoed. "Okay, have you been to the cops?"

"Yes. Before we called the alarm company, who called you, I called them. They already know I have a protection order, but I wanted to update them. They are keeping an eye out."

Nick shook his head, this sure wasn't what he expected when he brought her out here. He'd figured something was going on, but this? Plus he knew he didn't have the entire story, but both of them had had enough for today. Imagining this mousy little thing had been a stunning redhead that had an entitled amazing life was less challenging than it could have been. He'd seen something, some spark, something that had attracted him to her. His type had always been the feisty spunky ones aching to be tamed and dominated, but only for a short time, till they acted up again. Taming was the fun part, but never spirit squelching. Just a bit of male domination many of them seemed aching for. He'd never want to tame one completely. He'd always want that spark, that edge, that temper only a look from him could quell and only sometimes.

This story, though.

"How's the bottom?" he asked her and felt delighted to see a blush come over her cheeks. Next time, those pants would come down and he'd be able to watch the other ones blush, too. He'd be looking forward to that, and other things. That thought made him smile. He stroked her arm again and noticed how she instinctively cuddled next to him.

"It hurts," she whined. "Why did you do that?"

"You needed it, and it worked," he said.

"I didn't like it."

"But you needed it," he said, gently. "You feel better now, don't you?"

She shook her hair and her brown hair fell around her face in a way that delighted him. "Maybe," she confessed. "I still didn't like it."

"You aren't supposed to like it during, but after it's over, you will like the results. The way it makes you feel better, and calmer."

She shook her head again and he heard her stomach growl. "When have you eaten last?" She shrugged and he pulled her over his lap and swatted her a few times while she squealed, but seemed to realize he was playing because she didn't struggle. "Then I must save the Damsel from a fate worse than an empty belly. Do you eat real food?"

"Real food as opposed to what?" she asked him and stood up as he did while rubbing her bottom.

"Oh you know, all the new diet things I can't keep up with, keto, gluten free, vegetarian, or do you eat real food?" He watched her as she kept trying to rub the sting from her behind and wondered if she knew how hot that was. He wasn't going to tell her, she might stop.

"Yeah. You bought me beef kabobs, remember?"

He walked over to the kitchen area and wondered why she affected him the way she did? He knew he wasn't bad looking and had a job that attracted groupies. But this one, who was going to be a handful one way or another, just was different. Why? He'd worry about it later. Right now, he'd feed them both.

"How can I help?" she asked and he handed her a peeler and a couple potatoes. "You can have a seat and peel these, thanks," he said. He only had a few things he could make, and this meal was one of them.

"I'll just stand up if it's okay with you," she told him with a hint of sass he enjoyed hearing. She did feel better, from either the confession or the spanking, he wasn't certain which, but he felt weirdly glad he got to be a part of seeing some sauciness in her. Fixing things, as his dad always told him, was what a real man did. He helped. He wasn't part of the problem, he was the solution to problems, especially the female kind of problems. A real man made things better, and Nick grew up trying to be the man his father was.

"So where's your mom coming from?" he asked while they were working.

"She lives and works up in the northern Chicago area," Beth said. "That's where we were before we moved here."

"And she didn't come but all three of you did?" He knew she'd explained it but he found it hard to believe in a crisis she wouldn't have moved with her three children.

Beth smiled. "My mom lives and breathes her work. I'm surprised she's coming now. I bet she probably has a year of vacation time saved up and I imagine she won't stay two days. Being at the hospital is all she ever really wants."

"I understand that," he said. "We have a lot of those people at the fire department too. Personally, I think having a life outside of work makes you a better worker."

"I used to have a life," Beth said, very softly. "I was looking forward to getting it back."

"We aren't going to let one person take that from you," Nick said, almost fiercely before he realized he said 'we'. Were they a we? He'd only known her a few days. However, the attraction was undeniable. Plus, he was always a sucker for a damsel in distress as well as a feisty female with a smart mouth, who were often one and the same but didn't realize it till a warm bottom brought it to their attention.

The attraction had been there from the start when she'd fluttered those huge green eyes open. They'd look good with red hair. Maybe he could talk her into letting it go natural. "I assume your dad is no longer in the picture?"

She shook her head, and then said, "It is terrifying knowing he's in town. I'm scared for Joni, too. Last time he put me in the hospital for three days, and then dragged me through a horrific trial. I'm not wild about repeating either one of those things again." He took the potatoes away from her, rinsed them off, cut them, and put them in the pot of boiling water.

"The peels can go in the composter, over there," he pointed.

"Do you garden?" she asked.

He shrugged. "Just a couple things. Some tomatoes and peppers, that kind of thing. I don't have time for much more. You?"

Beth shook her head. "Not really. Joni is learning to, though. Our neighbor Hank is a Master Gardener and a really green thumb, so he's trying to teach her when they aren't fighting. But I don't like to be out that much."

Nick winced at how limited her life had been up till now. She'd just started feeling safe, and now this. He vowed to help, do what he could to change that. He'd do more to that guy than put him over his knee, for sure. Too bad public whippings weren't still a thing. There would be a grim satisfaction in seeing that.

He put some pre-packaged chicken fried steaks in the pan and pulled out the biscuits from the oven while she stirred the gravy and mashed the potatoes. Within minutes they were eating.

"You're a good cook," she told him.

"Not really, just a couple things I do well, and you helped," he said.

"I did," she said. "I'm an amazing potato peeler and masher."

"I bet you have other skills," he said but noticed her smile fade and her eyes dart away. What had he said? Well, whatever it was, she had shut down pretty fast.

"I need to get home," she said. "Thank you for lunch. Let me help you clean up."

She stood up and started to clear the small table while he tried to decide what to do. She'd probably had enough for today.

"You're welcome," he said, as he ran hot water in the sink and started washing dishes while she cleared. "Some plastic stuff up in that cabinet for leftovers."

She seemed to relax while working, so even though his grandma would have had a fit, he let the company help clean up. Then he'd take her home, double check the locks and probably spend the night at the fire house. He didn't want to be all the way out here if something did happen. He'd call his buddy, Graham at the station too, and see when he was working and give him a heads up. He'd really like to be sleeping with her, well, at her house, tonight. He had a suspicion that wouldn't go over well though. At least not yet.

One thing he did know, though, was this adorable not really a mouse, spankable little woman was in his life for a while at least. He didn't need to understand why. Some days it was good to be a male and just not have to overthink everything.

Beth looked around the living room. It was ready. Was it? Could it ever be really ready for their mother? Joni and Hank had driven to meet her at the airport, and Joni had texted two hours ago that they had her in the car. That meant they would be here soon.

Beth had made her mother's favorite summer meal of a fresh fruit salad and a light chicken wrap stuffed with vegetables and it was waiting for her arrival. Sydney's room had been cleaned well, and new, washed sheets were on the bed, the bathroom had been scrubbed and the floors all buffed. She and Joni weren't slobs but often let the house look lived in. They were both happy with it. But their mother? Not so much. She liked things to be operating room clean and that was a challenging standard to live up to. They didn't have a staff or sterilizing equipment. It looked like a house that people lived in, not a sterile environment.

This was her mother, she reminded herself. She loved her and the only reason she was coming, leaving her job, which was all but unheard of, was her. She was here to make sure one of her children was okay. Not to inspect the corners of the house.

They would get in fairly late, eat and probably would go to bed. Then all day tomorrow, they would have to find something to do. There was an antique mall on the edge of town that she'd like to go to, but doubted it would interest their mother. She picked up her phone and called her little sister.

"Beth!" Came the delighted answer. "Thank you for pharmaceutical studies! My brain is on overload."

"Oh, drugs!" Beth teased. "Sounds like fun."

"Yeah, only if you are a horse," Sydney said. "What's up? You doing okay?"

"I just thought I'd let you know Mom is on her way here in case you want to stop studying about drugging horses and run on down for a day or two, let her tell you how to live instead of me."

"Wait, what? Mom's coming? Why? What happened? Mom doesn't leave work."

Beth grimaced. Should she tell her? "Apparently some joker called her and told her I was in an accident and she needs to come see me with her own eyes."

"Well, there's this fancy new thing now called video chat," Sydney said. "Bethie, was it him?"

"Probably," Beth said. "Just thought I'd say something to you. You know."

"I know. Beth, you be safe. Keep in touch, okay? I know I'm bad about it, but the last year here is just crazy."

"Thought about where you will work when you get out?"

"Oh, a couple places. Trying to make sure I pass first, though."

"Passing would be good, but no one is as smart as you. Well, maybe Joni's boyfriend, she teased.

"I don't know, he's dating Joni, isn't he?" Sydney said back. "Seriously though, you take care. As soon as I start applying to places, I'll let you know."

"I will. And I doubt you will have to apply, I imagine they will be beating down your door."

"Yup, I'm that amazing. Bye, Beth, talk to you soon. Let me know how Mom's visit goes."

"Well, if you are sure you can't come," Beth said. "Bye, Syd."

Hanging up, she glanced at the time. They should be here soon. Nick would be getting off work soon, but said he wouldn't come over tonight. It was family night, but he'd be around and wanted to treat them all to lunch tomorrow. So that would break up the day a little. Then they could do a ride around the lake. And? She couldn't take her mom to the batting cages. A walk around the square? It was very sad when you didn't really know what your mom liked to do in her spare time because you never saw her have much. Any? Looking back over her childhood, the only thing she really remembered her mom doing was working, coming home, talking to them a while and going to bed. Surely she had some kind of life?

Other doctors did. She remembered seeing her pediatrician at her softball games with her own daughter. Had her mom ever come to hers? Did it matter? Not really, she was an adult and her mom loved them all, they knew she did. They all graduated from college with no student loan debt like many of their friends were still struggling with. Syd got accepted into vet school and she suspected part of that was because of who their mother was. Vet schools were hard to get into!

Picking up the can of dusting spray, she started re-polishing the tables. Might as well.

"So where are we going for lunch?" Joni asked as they all headed toward her car the next afternoon.

"I'm sure it's somewhere lovely." Their mom was dressed casually, in leggings and a light tunic top with sneakers. She was used to wearing scrubs, she said, and fancy clothes just weren't her thing. It had been a long morning and Beth was looking forward to seeing Nick.

"We're going to meet Nick at the Running Water. You know how to get there, Joni? Oh, there's Hank. Is he coming?"

"Oh, yeah," Joni said in a way that made Beth grin. Her sister needed reinforcement too. Her smile quickly faded. She was trying very hard to fake happy go lucky, unstressed and doing just fine, even great! However, it wasn't really working very well. Her palm had ridges where her fingernails kept biting into it. Poor thing. The pain helped her focus though and remember to smile. She'd need stitches by the time this was over. What was over? Either the weekend or the suspense of the unknown, and who knew when that would be? At least her mom would be leaving tomorrow afternoon. She could count down the hours to that. To this situation being over? She wasn't sure if it ever would be.

But for now, she was plastering on the grin and doing the carefree thing, and really, she felt safe with her mom around. No one messed with her.

Hank walked through the fence gate between their two houses to their driveway. "Hey, Joni, Bethie, good morning, Doc Denny. You sleep well?"

"I certainly did," their mom, Denise, who for some reason went by Doc Denny, said. "How about you, Hank? Looking forward to spending an afternoon with my two girls and their friends."

"Oh, I'm good." He turned to Joni and said, "Talked to Nick, he's meeting us at the Running Water, want me to drive?"

"I absolutely do," Joni said and Beth wondered if they would manage to control their legendary volatility during lunch with a common bond of 'keep mamma happy'. Even Hank had seemed a bit shook when they'd arrived over an hour later than planned last night. They'd eaten the supper that Beth had prepared and her mother didn't say a word, which meant she liked it, while she explained her fight with the state police. They claimed to have never called her and offered to trace the phone that made the call, saying it could be harassment. She still hadn't heard back from them and assumed it was put on the back burner. Once she had time, she said, she'd follow up. While Beth knew she probably would never have time, she felt bad for the police if she did.

It was going to be an interesting lunch.

She got in the back seat with Joni while their mom and Hank took the front. Did she feel nervous about Nick meeting her mom? A little. Mostly she wanted him to like her for some reason, she wasn't worried that her mom would like Nick. Most people did, but hoped he wouldn't get the third degree like Hank apparently got on the way home from the airport.

However, this was her mother. Who knew what she'd think was an appropriate subject? She smiled as they pulled into the parking lot and she saw Nick's truck with the handsome fireman leaning against it. She'd fallen for him way too fast, she knew. She wasn't a damsel, though and worried that she'd lean on him too much too soon. But right now, leaning was fine. Getting through lunch with Mother was the only goal.

He began walking over to them with that gorgeous Nick grin on his face, and walking straight up to their mother. "Hello, I'm Nick and you must be Dr. Montgomery. I'm so glad to meet you. Beth, Joni, Hank." He gave them a nod.

"Hello, Nick. Aren't you the handsome one? Call me Dr. Denny, please. I can't wait to get to know you. Let's go eat." She linked her arm in his and headed to the door. "Come along, girls."

The girls came along. Beth heard Hank whisper to Joni, "Guess I know where I rank now."

"Yeah, you're just a genius. Nick is a firefighter. No comparison."

"Sorry about that," Hank said and Beth bit back an almost unfaked smile.

Almost two hours later they walked out, after a surprisingly interesting and easy lunch. Dr. Denny had regaled everyone with stories of life in the ER, she'd only interrogated Nick for a short time and seemed pleased with his answers. The food was good and Beth felt happy as to how it went.

"Walk me to my truck, Beth," he said after he said goodbye, and she gladly slipped away for a minute. He took her hand and that made her overly happy, just to feel his touch. "How'd I do?" he asked when they were out of ear shot. "Your mom is a force of nature, isn't she?"

Nodding her head, Beth agreed with him. "She was actually on very very good behavior. She only sent her food back twice and critiqued the poor waitress for her uniform once. The decor was simply scorned and not disdained."

"Constitutes good behavior in my book," he nodded. "Hate to leave you alone with her, but I've got an appointment across town and am running late."

"I just bet you do. Thank you for coming, Nick."

"I'll be over tomorrow," he said, and climbed in his truck as she turned to walk back to where Hank had already started the car.

Looking across the parking lot, she saw a man standing under a tree. Her body reacted immediately, knowing who it was. Nick was already gone, and she couldn't move or breathe for what felt like an hour, but knew it couldn't be. Dragging her eyes away, she hurried to the car and got in. When she looked back, he was gone. Had she imagined it? No. She knew she hadn't. Her body, brain and fear instinct knew she hadn't. He'd been there, but now he was gone. She wasn't going to ruin anyone else's day, but she'd be extra cautious.

———

"Beth, it has been two weeks. You haven't been out of the house since Mom left. Nick's been over every day since begging you to go out with him."

"He hasn't begged," Beth protested. "Just asked a couple times."

Joni sighed in a way Beth knew meant she was disgusted. "Go out to dinner with him tonight! Go breathe some air that isn't in here!" Joni put her hands on her hips and Beth scowled at her.

"I'm not hungry."

"Do I care if you are hungry? No. I swear, if you don't get

out of here for a few hours I'm calling Mom and asking her to come back. Do we want that? No, we absolutely do not! But I will!"

Beth sighed. "No, we both had quite enough of Mom. I can't believe you'd call her."

"Maybe I'm desperate," Joni teased. "I want to go hang out with Hank and not have to worry about you."

"I am fine in my office," Beth said. "Don't go putting that on me."

"Beth. Go out with the man. He's desperate for a little alone time with you."

"He is not," she protested.

"Beth, seriously. Do you trust your own judgement when it comes to men?"

"Ouch," Beth said as mildly as she could.

"Really. Eli was your only serious boyfriend and that only lasted a few months. Take it from me - Nick is a good guy and he's crazy about you," Joni said. "Please, just once. Go out to dinner with him."

Beth shook her head stubbornly, wincing, she never said his name and didn't like hearing it. She got up and went back to her office. Sinking down in her office chair, she folded her arms and spun around a couple times. What was wrong with Joni? She knew what was going on. Just because nothing had happened in two weeks didn't mean nothing would. He knew where she was and he was just waiting. Sure, she'd been in shock and actually had gone with Nick that one time, but really, had it been smart? No. Did anything happen? Also no. Well but for the fact he'd spanked her into spilling the story she'd vowed to never tell again. What was with that? Why had she allowed it? Not like she'd had any choice, she half smiled at that thought.

Did she want it to be repeated? What repeated? The relaxation she felt with him, the freedom from tension, worry and fear she felt when she was with him? Yeah. she wouldn't mind that. Even though she couldn't forget that he'd spanked her, which she also didn't want repeated. In retrospect though, it was a little hot. The fact he'd just taken over, decided to do it, and then just did it. Dominating, but not domineering. There was a fine difference in her mind, and he knew right where that line was. Sure, he was showing up here every day, and asking her to go out, but wasn't pressuring her. He sat, talked, and just made her feel at ease. Maybe she would go out with him today. Just for a little while, but not to his cabin! She knew what happened when they went to the cabin! He fed one end and paddled the other. Nope. No cabin time.

She heard voices in the kitchen and figured it was either him or Hank, so went out the office door and down the hall. There he was, in all his Nick glory, looking hot and eating a cookie. She suddenly wanted... cookies, very badly.

He looked up and smiled at her. "Good, jeans and sneakers, just what you need. Grab your purse or whatever you need. Come on, we're going out."

He said it like she hadn't turned him down every day for two weeks now. Just like he expected her to. Well, fine. She'd show him. "Okay."

Turning around, she went back to her office and grabbed her purse. Catching a glimpse of herself in the hall mirror, she frowned at her roots. Well, nothing she could do about it today. If she even wanted to.

"Did she say okay?" she overheard Joni ask.

"What can I say? I'm persuasive," Nick said. "Besides, she's got to be going stir crazy in here. I would be."

"She feels safe in here," Joni said.

Beth felt a little annoyed that they were talking about her as if she wasn't right in the other room. Truth was though, she did feel safe at home. She also felt safe with Nick. However, if he was out there somewhere and decided to target Nick, well.

That stopped her in her tracks. She and Joni both carried pepper spray and a very loud alarm they could set off with the touch of a finger. What did he have? Yeah, that wasn't fair to him.

Coming back in the kitchen, without her purse, she said, "I don't think this is a good idea."

Nick grinned at her, then calmly stood up, grabbed her, and threw her over his shoulder as if it were something he did every day. "Hey! Put me down!"

"Nah, you need some fresh air. See you later, Joni. I'll have her home early."

"Have fun!" Joni said through her laughter. "Bye!"

"I can walk!" Beth informed him. "Put me down!"

"I know you can walk," he said as if she weren't having a tantrum. "The question is, will you walk?"

Would she? "I will! I promise!"

"You better. If I put you down, you march yourself right to my truck, you understand? And you know what will happen if you don't."

"I will! I will!" Last thing she wanted was the neighbors seeing her over his shoulder.

"Okay, Damsel." He put her down on her feet and grinned at her. "Head to the truck."

Would he have spanked her on the porch, in front of the neighbors and any random people driving by? Somehow she thought he might. Not chancing it was a very good idea. She moved toward the truck, after throwing him a look. "You are lucky you are cute," Beth informed him. "Otherwise you wouldn't get away with so much."

"True fact," he said, opening the door for her. "Climb your little self right on in."

Bracing for the expected butt smack, she smiled when it landed. Dang him, anyway. He slammed the truck door behind her and she thought for a second about waiting till he was on his side and sprinting out. Nah. It did feel good to be out. The sun was out, shining on the trees and flowers, everything looked so bright and clear. Today had to be a good day. Nothing bad could happen when it was so perfect out. She heaved a happy sigh, glad she'd decided to go out.

"I didn't grab my purse, by the way. What are we doing?" she asked him.

"You'll see," he said.

"That's mysterious."

"I'm cute and mysterious. What more could one man possibly be?" He turned the truck down the main highway.

"Forthcoming?" she suggested, but decided it didn't really matter. "You know, if he sees us out, you could be targeted."

"Is that why you wouldn't go out with me again?" he asked. "And here I thought it was the good paddling I gave you."

"Well, that too," she told him. "But really, it isn't fair to you to get involved with me."

"It isn't?" He gave her a glance.

"I come with baggage," she said.

"Most women do," he agreed.

"Mine is worse."

"You thinking I can't handle you and your baggage?"

"I am practically perfect in every way. It's the other stuff. It isn't fair to you to, Nick! Is that a batting cage?"

He pulled into a parking lot. "Yup. Batting cage and a rock wall. I figured you had some pent up energy."

Beth felt like drooling. The thing she missed most about her old life, besides her old life, was softball. She'd always felt at home on the field and spent many, many hours in the batting cage. "Do we get to play?" she asked him.

As he put the truck in park, and smiled, she threw her arms around him. "Thank you! I'm so excited!"

"I'm glad," he said. "Too bad I had to twist your arm. Maybe you will learn to trust me."

"Don't hold your breath," she said, as she almost jumped out of the truck in her eagerness to get to the batting cage. "I didn't even know this was here."

"It's new," he said. "There is going to be a water park over there in the next year or two."

"In our little town?" she said. "I can't believe it."

It wasn't long before she was at bat. It had been a while, so she did a few warm up swings. The first crack of the bat gave her shivers all the way to her toes. It had been too long. Automatically, she reached up to adjust her not there ball cap, but grinned. Hey, this was living.

"Fifteen out of twenty," Nick said. "How come you aren't in the majors?"

"Ask them," she said. "Twenty more?"

"You'll be sore tomorrow," he warned. "Why not?"

That set, she only did twelve of twenty. Her out of shape shoulders were getting sore. Did she care? Not really.

"That felt so good," she told him. "Thank you for bringing me. Your turn?" Nick shook his head. "I'm worn out just watching you."

Beth giggled and that felt good too. "Thank you again," she said, and impulsively hugged him again. Okay, that felt even better. He was a good hugger. Sighing, she nestled into him. He felt like home. Much different than he who wouldn't be named. He didn't hug well, more standoffish. Not really cold, but well, not Nick. She liked a Nick hug, she decided. "I loved the batting cage. Thank you."

"You did? That's good to know, because I couldn't tell," he smiled at her and her frozen Grinch heart melted just a little tiny bit. Yeah, she was easy. Give her a ball bat and there she was, a puddle of mush.

"I better go home now," she murmured. *Before someone sees*

us together. It would be safer that way. However, she was having a really good time and it felt so good to get out of the house.

"Why?" he asked her.

"Well, mainly because you can't top that, so party is over. Might as well head home before I'm bored silly." She yawned loudly and obnoxiously just to see his smile.

He nodded. "Batting practice is the highlight of your day?"

Beth laughed. "My day? Nah, that was actually the highlight of the last couple years."

"I'm sorry about that," he said. "We'll have to see what we can do to change that."

"Nick! This is not a good time for me to be changing my life! He's in town somewhere, just biding his time, waiting. I don't want you involved in that. Too many people rely on you, your job is too important."

"You and your life are important too," he said. "You planning to sit home in your little office for the rest of your life?"

She shrugged as they walked to the truck. "Look what happened the first time I decided to go out in public."

"That is unfortunate," he said, opening the truck door for her, and giving her the smack on the butt again. She wondered if he'd be around long enough for her to get used to him doing that. Sure, she expected it, but still that wasn't the same as being used to it. She kind of liked it but wasn't sure why.

"I know. My life is nothing but a series of misfortunate adventures. It didn't used to be this way, though."

"Tell me about old Beth. The one before. What was she like?"

Beth smiled. "She was a handful. Cocky and very sure of herself. A little over confident and certain everyone loved her and thought she was great."

"And did they?" He started the truck.

Beth shrugged. "I rather doubt every single person

thought as highly of me as I thought of myself. I really thought I could do no wrong and was totally justified in the things I did."

"So what do you think now?"

"I think I was sort of an asshole," she said. "I thought I knew it all and most people were beneath me. One of the perks of being told how beautiful, smart and accomplished you are since you were a kid."

"Is it? What did your sisters think of that?"

"I didn't care. I just accepted it as my due. That's why I–" She hesitated and looked at him. "Why I changed the way I look. Cut my hair, colored it, wear the baggy clothes and big sunglasses. I don't remember the last time I dressed up. No, that isn't true. I remember it too well. The day I ruined his life. I mean, you have to look good to show up the wifey and ruin someone's life, don't you?"

"It hasn't really come up in my life," he said, parking the car in front of a walking path.

"Lucky you." She shrugged, they got out and he grabbed her hand. Then smiled as his fingers tightened on hers. "I looked really good. Then spent the next day in bed eating chocolate and bawling. He showed up one night and the rest is history. I cut my hair off as soon as the bruises healed enough, and colored my hair."

"Aren't you tired of it?" he asked as they got closer to the pond. She saw a little bridge over on one corner and deftly steered them over there.

"Tired of hiding? Yeah. That day you and I worked at the event in the park, that was the first real thing I'd done since we moved here, I think I told you that. I was sick and tired of being sick and tired. Then look where that got me. It is so beautiful out here."

"It is," he agreed.

"So tell me about you," she said as they stopped in the

middle of the bridge. "You know everything about me and I know nothing about you but that you spank too hard and are a firefighter."

"I don't spank too hard," he assured her with a squeeze of his hand. "I spank just right."

"Huh," she said. "Yeah, you just keep telling yourself that."

"Okay," he said agreeably. "Not much to tell. I'm the middle of five brothers, grew up a few hours west of here. Mom and Dad were both firefighters, one of my brothers and I are too. I worked in the same town I grew up in till I wanted something different, and started applying around. There was an opening here. More money, close to the lake and there was a rumor there were a lot of pretty girls here."

"Never been married? No kids?" she asked.

"Nope and nope," he said. "Beth, what's wrong?"

She pointed, feeling frozen. There. There he was. With a redhead. Of course.

Chapter 4

Beth sat outside the townhouse, working up her courage. She could do this. She had to do this. There was no option. Desperately wishing she had half the confidence of her former self, she balled her hands into fists and determinedly got out of her car to wait.

If the last week was a regular routine, then Miranda would be leaving for work in a few minutes. What was she going to say? All the carefully rehearsed words flew out of her head when she saw the redhead, really strawberry blonde up close, walk out the door, heading to her small, elegant luxury car. How did she keep that so clean?

Taking a deep shaking breath, she managed to call out as she walked toward her, "Miranda? Miranda? Hi! I'm Beth! Your brother is engaged to my friend Jordyn." She waved as if she were friendly. She was friendly. This was a good thing.

"Is Ben okay?" Miranda asked her, walking closer in her tight powder blue blazer, tight pencil skirt, and very high heels. How did she walk in those things? The skirt or the heels? Well, she used to do it without a thought, she reminded herself, and then dance all night in them. Just took getting used to, or the leg strength of hours at the gym. .

"Ben is fine," she assured her. "That's not why I'm here."

Miranda flipped her long hair back and looked at her so coolly, Beth felt her extremities begin to freeze. "How can I help you?"

"I was walking at the park the other day and saw you with Eli." Okay, she got that out.

"Excuse me?" Yeah, that was utter ice queen. Beth tried not to shiver.

"I used to date Eli," she started.

"You want him back? Honey, no one can get stolen unless they want to be. I had no idea he was dating…" Miranda looked her up and down and said, *"you"* in a way Beth knew wasn't a compliment.

Everyone who had worked with her admired Miranda's work ethic and her house and office designs, her knowledge of all things code and requirements, but everyone also said they felt a little chilled and less than after a meeting with her. Miranda was just superior. She knew it and after you talked to her, you knew it, too. Beth half wondered if she came across that way back in the day. That felt disconcerting, but was not why she was here, today, though.

"We broke up a couple of years ago. I moved away and he moved here to, well, umm, because of me."

"Has he called you? Come by? Asked you out? Because he's done all those things to me."

Yeah, he came by once, broke into my house and left me a present. She couldn't say that though. She had no real proof, even though she knew. "Yeah, he's attracted to you. You, me and the ex-wife are all redheads. He has a type."

"And when he got a glimpse of you he decided you weren't his type or weren't a redhead? Really, Beth, I'm not sure why you are here but I am going to be late if I don't get going."

Miranda moved toward her car again. Beth knew that despite all her good qualities, Miranda was always late to everything. Apparently she liked to keep people waiting and to make an entrance.

"Miranda, he put me in the hospital."

That stopped her in her tracks. "What?"

"He beat me up and put me in the hospital. I was in there three days."

"He beat you up." Miranda said it as if it wasn't actually a thing.

"He did. Google it. And him. I pressed charges and everything."

"And he was found not guilty?"

"Legal technicality. It didn't go to court." Beth felt her heart sink. Miranda wasn't believing her, but maybe she would Google him later. Why wouldn't she? "I just wanted to warn you."

"I appreciate your interest, but I can take care of myself," Miranda got in her car and sped away without a backwards glance.

That didn't go well. Beth tried to stop her hands from shaking as she got back into her car, well, Joni's car. One day, she'd have to get one of her own. Especially if she moved.

Sighing, she headed back toward the house. What good would it do to move? He'd just find her again. No. She had to settle this one way or another. Fingering the pepper spray in her pocket made her feel a little safer. Joni had gone with Hank to a ball game at the middle school, so she had the car for a few hours. What should she do? She drove around idly for a few minutes, then gave up. She'd go to Jordyn's for some dessert for tonight and then head home and work. Why not? It was a gorgeous Southern Illinois day, so why not lock herself in the office instead of going to the lake or something. Nick was at work and he'd be furious if he knew she went to see

Miranda without him. He'd flat out told her not to. Well, he was going to find out. She'd tell him. She knew what secrets did to people. They got your new fling walking up to your wife and getting you divorced and fired. She wasn't going to be part of that, even though he'd probably spank her for it. What was it with him and his obsession with spanking her? It was beyond weird and nothing she looked forward to, at all.

She had to do it, had to tell him, though. Nick thought the only thing it would do would be antagonize Eli. He might be right, but Miranda needed to know. To be safe. Would he do it again, though? Maybe he only did it to people who ruined his life and everyone else would be just fine with him? Why was he in town?

Nick had called his buddy Sheriff Graham after she'd seen Eli, but he'd told her that as long as he didn't come near her and violate the protection order, he wasn't breaking any laws. Beth dreaded the day he did break those laws, though. She almost wished he would, and just get it over with. This living in suspense was killing her. She just hoped he wouldn't. She had also been informed that she couldn't confront him, even if she wanted to do that, which she'd thought about but didn't think she could. The protection order apparently worked both ways. Legally, she couldn't go near him either.

Parking across the street from Baking Memories, Jordyn's shop, she decided to walk around the little park before she went in and loaded up on sugary sweetness. It was the right thing to do. Inhaling the sweet summer air, she saw the unmistakable form of Jordyn's fiancé and Miranda's brother Ben, walking in her direction. The man was built like a mountain. Had Miranda already talked to him? He was probably just going to see Jordyn. He might not even recognize her. He'd come over and renovated the bathroom in the house, but it had been a while and her goal was to blend in, after all.

"Hey, Beth," he rumbled. So maybe she wasn't as good at

blending as she thought.

"Good morning, Ben," she said, adjusting her sunglasses. "Heading to the bakery?" Should she tell Ben about Eli? Probably.

"Yup, but I'm glad I ran into you."

"Need a logo designed?" She hoped that was what he needed.

"Nope. I got a phone call from my sister. Randy tells me you and her current friend, who I'm not fond of by the way, used to be a thing and you are spreading some gossip around. Any truth to any of it?" He leaned against the nearest tree and waited.

"Oh, that." Okay, so that was taken out of her hands. She would have to tell him now. What else could she do?

"I don't gossip," she said. "It's true. Google it." Did no one in this town use the internet? He made a motion as if she should continue. So she took a deep breath.

"Short story, we broke up, he came over and beat me up. Then apparently followed me down here. He's dangerous."

"You've lived here a couple years now," Ben said, slowly. "He just now find you?"

Beth nodded. "Apparently."

"Coincidence?" he asked.

She shook her head. Ben nodded and said slowly, "I see. Thanks for the heads up. You be careful, okay?"

"I will. Thanks."

Now she felt even worse. Was Eli really dangerous? Of course he was, but maybe as long as no one else blew up his life, he wouldn't hospitalize them. Yes, she knew she had some niggling guilt over what she'd done. The therapist she'd seen for a year told her that was normal. There was no excuse for it. It wasn't his wife's fault he was a lying, cheating piece of scum. His son didn't deserve to lose his dad. She'd made sure he lost everything and she'd done it on purpose and out of spite. How was that not as bad as what he'd done? Well, because. What she did was mental, and his was physical? That didn't sit well with her, but neither did the hospital bills or the therapy after. The moving and the living in fear.

She strode around the park, hiking her pants more than once. Yes, she needed a belt. Or she could just eat more pastry and pasta That sounded like a better idea.

As she got around the edge of the square, she saw Ben leaving the bakery and felt glad she didn't have to run into him again. There had been enough talk today. Hopefully, she wasn't going to have to discuss it again with Jordyn. If she did, she'd go home and lock herself in her office for a week while eating cupcakes.

Getting closer, once again, she smiled at her design hanging on the bakery wall. She missed design. But the insurance job was anonymous and safe. Even though she was neither anymore, she reminded herself.

"Hello, Beth," Jordyn smiled from behind the counter. "Good to see you!" Ben mustn't have said anything to her, Beth decided. Good. She had told that story enough for the day.

"Good morning, Jordyn. How's business?"

"This is my morning lull," Jordyn said, cheerfully. "We are slammed every morning from 6:30 to about 9 then it slows down till about eleven when people start coming in again."

"Busy is good," Beth said. "Heard from Lucy lately?" She told her the order.

"Yeah, didn't Joni tell you? We all got together the other night, just a girls' night. It was fun! Lucy is just Lucy, you know? She's a blast."

Once again, Beth felt a pang. She really needed her own group of friends. Expecting Joni's friends to be hers wasn't fair or right to any of them. Still, it hurt they never even considered her and she wasn't going to lie about it.

After paying, she took the box and headed to her car. Looking down the street, she saw a sign, in more than one way. Putting the box in the car, she locked the door, took a deep breath and with a determined stride, headed back down the street. Screw it. Why not?

Nick left the station and headed to his truck. Four days off and he had a good idea how he was going to spend them. He was going to take Beth home to meet his mama. She'd told him she had vacation time coming, his hometown was only about four hours away. They'd go down, spend the night and come back the next day. Or maybe a couple days. It would be good to get away for a little while. He smiled, realizing he still considered where he grew up home. Well, that was normal. His mom planned to retire next year and she and his dad were in the process of moving to the country. His dad who'd retired a few years ago, already spent most of his time out there fixing up the house and outbuildings. Maybe he'd swing a hammer while he was there.

He hoped Beth could be talked into it fairly easily. Sure, he could throw her over his shoulder and force her to, but it would be more enjoyable if she agreed. He'd go see her, then go home and pack an overnight bag and they could leave in the morning. After four twelves in a row, he knew he'd wear down fast if they left tonight. Even he needed his sleep.

He got to the house, rang the bell and waved, since he knew Beth would look at the camera before she opened the door. He was right. When she opened it, he looked at her trying not to gasp. "Excuse me, ma'am," he said politely. "I'm looking for a little brunette about your size. She used to live here?"

"You like it?" she asked and did a little twirl. Instead of

her baggy jeans and oversize shirt she usually wore, she was barefoot in a soft, well-fitting sundress that made her look amazing, but not as amazing as her now dark red hair. Auburn? It suited her, as did the dress. The bare feet and her legs were not bad at all.

"Love it. Got a hot date?" Maybe she did. That thought did not make him happy. Not one little bit.

"Just felt like a change. I'm tired of hiding in plain sight. He already knows where I am and living my life in fear is exhausting. I want a life again."

"You don't know how glad I am to hear that," he said, and pulled her into a kiss. Yeah. this was more like it. He'd known this was in her, the feisty, sassy redhead. The mousy little damsel tried to hide her but she refused to be hidden and that was a good thing.

She melted into his arms, molding her body to his, then stiffened, and he stopped.

"What?"

"I need to tell you something."

This didn't sound good. "I won't lie to you," she continued. "I know what lying gets."

"Okay. Go ahead," he said, as she took his hand and led him into the kitchen.

"Well, Joni was out with Hank today and so I had the car."

He nodded. "She still gone?"

"Yeah. They won't be home till late. They went to a ball game and now are going to the drive-in that just opened a couple towns over. She just called me."

"Go on," he said, sitting down in a kitchen chair while she did the same. He noticed her fingers balled into her palms. A sure sign she was stressed.

"Well, I drove over and talked to Miranda."

Damn. "Beth, you didn't."

She nodded. "I did and I'm not sorry. She needed to know. I don't really know her well, but no one deserves, well—"

"That's not the point. The point is, I asked you not to. What if he'd been with her? That protection order goes both ways. You can't go near him either. You want to be in trouble?"

She shook her now red head and he couldn't get over how much it just suited her, complimented her coloring and face. This must be close to her natural color. Beth sat in her chair, staring down and looked like just what she was. An adorable girl who knew she was in trouble and about to get a spanking. She had one fist balled up and the other twisting the fabric of her little sundress.

"Well, you are in trouble. Bring me that wooden spoon over there."

She hesitated for a minute while he waited. "Do I have to?"

"Yes. Do it now."

She didn't ask again. Apparently she needed what he was about to give her. He vowed to do a good job, and one, teach her to be safe, and listen to the rules he'd set in place, and two, to give her what she seemed to desire to get her guilt absolved.

She brought it over and handed it to him. "I'm sorry," she said.

"I imagine you will be a lot sorrier in a few minutes. Now, get that pretty little rear over my lap."

He heard her breath hitch, but she did as she was told. He liked the way she felt over his knee, liked the way she did as she was told.

"Now, you know why you are getting this, right?"

"Yes, sir," she said, squirming, as if she were trying to get comfortable or maybe second thinking her position.

He used his hand and smacked her over the pretty dress and made her start. "So tell me."

"Tell you?" He smacked her other cheek and felt her jerk again. He'd give her a nice little hand warm up before he lifted that skirt and used the spoon. As much as she carried on last time, this one would certainly get her attention.

"You will be safe under my watch, do you understand?" He swatted her twice more and she wiggled.

"Yes, sir," she said, fairly meekly, he thought. Well, he'd get some fight in her and make sure she was good and sorry. Last thing he wanted to do was scrape her up off the sidewalk because she was going around half-cocked, warning people or whatever she thought she was doing. It was a good thing they were leaving town for a few days. Oh, he'd forgotten to tell her that. Well, there would be time enough after her paddling.

"Ow!" she whimpered.

"Hold still and take your spanking like a good girl," he told her. "You deserve this and you know it."

"I can't! It hurts." She wiggled but so far had kept her hands down. Well, that would change as soon as he picked up the wooden spoon here in a minute. There would be no way she wouldn't try and cover her bottom then.

"We won't have this discussion again," he told her while he continued to smack her bottom while she wiggled and tried not to vocalize. That amused him. She could try to be stoic but he'd had naughty bottoms over his lap quite often and knew what he was doing. If she needed a good cathartic cry and be absolved of guilt, he could do that for her. It was almost his duty. She'd come to him asking him for just that, and he could deliver.

Finally he felt as if he'd warmed her little bottom up enough and grabbed the wooden spoon. "Let's get this bottom bare and start your spanking," he said lifting her dress while she reached back and grabbed at it.

"No! No! I'm done, I'll be good!"

Ignoring her protests, he said, "I don't think you are in any position to decide that, young lady. Now settle down."

"Yes, sir." He heard again, but noticed she couldn't stop clenching and unclenching her bottom cheeks under her barely there bikini panties as he lifted her skirt. Her rear looked nice and pink already.

"Let's see if we can make this little bottom match that hair, what do you say." He smacked the closest cheek with the spoon, watching the spot bloom from pink to white and back to pink as she let out a loud squeal. Good. She felt that.

He started a steady patter, singing *"Boot Scoot Boogie"* in his head. It always worked for a good rhythm of spanks on a tender female rear. Enough to keep up a good steady round of. smacks that built to a crescendo at the end. Nick knew he enjoyed giving a good well-needed spanking, and he also loved giving fun playful ones. Hopefully, she'd get one of those soon. Right now though he watched her little bottom jiggle with each smack and begin to turn a darker pink. Her whimpers began to turn into yelps and protests,

Wiggling, her bare feet began kicking and her arm flew back, almost knocking him in the face trying to block her probably aching bottom. Nothing he couldn't handle. He tipped her up, over just one knee, just a bit more to put her off balance so she had to hold herself up with at least one hand, then clamped her legs down with the other.

"Now, I have a good target. Let's get you good and spanked. You'll learn to listen to me when I tell you something."

She sobbed out a *no* that seemed to hang on forever while he ignored it. He'd know when she was done and she was far from it.

She'd hit a little panic spot though, and fought against him hard, trying to get away. It was actually kind of cute. Futile, but cute.

"Your bottom is getting blistered no matter how hard you fight," he told her. "You might as well settle down and accept your spanking like the naughty girl you were."

"I'm sorry!" she wailed.

What did she expect him to say? "Not as sorry as you are going to be." Of course, and swatted both thighs twice with the spoon which made her voice rise two octaves. Yeah, he was getting her attention. It didn't take long and her voice was breaking.

"You will remember this next time you don't do as you are told," he said, but wasn't sure she could hear him over her sobs and frantic efforts to get away. She probably had about all she needed for today. He gave her four more swats on her upper thighs that made her shriek, then tossed the spoon on the table, and gave her bright red bottom a quick, few rubs. Dang, it was hot. Hopefully, he hadn't gone overboard. Nah.

Nick allowed her to go down on her knees beside him and use his leg as a sobbing post. He patted her red head and stroked her back. He imagined she'd learned her lesson, felt a little better and felt relieved from some guilt, even though her bottom would be sore for a few days.

"I'm sorry," she said and sniffled while he looked around for a tissue. Nary a one in sight. Paper towels over on the counter but he couldn't reach them and he knew better than to leave a sobbing female alone. That never went well, so his pants would have to suffer until she felt up to moving. He could deal.

"I know you are," he told her, continuing to stroke her. "But you learned, didn't you?" She nodded her head and he watched the highlights bounce through her hair. Something about a redhead, he thought. He couldn't wait to take her home to Mama. "That's a good girl. And you know what we are going to do because you took your spanking so well?" She shook her head this time.

"You and I are going to skip town for a few days. Head on over to Zephyrhills and just do some relaxation." This time she shrugged and he realized she probably felt a little insecure after her spanking. "Come here, climb on my lap."

Doing as she was told, she noticeably winced as she settled there, but snaked her arms around his neck and pressed her face into his shoulder. "There, that feel better?" he asked patting her back.

She shrugged, and said, "Maybe. I don't know."

Hugging her close, he kissed her forehead and told her, "See. You're good. Think how much better it will be to get out of here for a few days. Away from the stress and worry. Just me and you, having a good time, eating some great food and taking it easy."

"I'm scared to leave," she said and lifted her still wet green eyes to his. "I haven't left this town since I got here. Even though I know he's in town, it just feels safer than leaving, you know?"

No. He didn't know. That made no sense to him at all, but he wasn't going to tell her that. "Do you feel safe with me?" he asked.

Her eyes didn't leave his as she said, "Yes. I do. Even if you make a point of making my rear sore. It hurts."

"Then trust I'll keep you safe and if you get scared, I'll bring you right back. But I bet you will be just fine once we get out of town."

"Okay," she said. "I'll believe you, and yes, it would be nice to get away. Maybe. Where are we going, what do I pack?" Then she looked around wildly, and jumped off his lap as they both heard the front door open.

"Beth, it's me. You home?"

Beth fled to the bathroom to wash her face, he assumed, as he heard Joni come through the living room, and he called out, "In the kitchen, Joni, it's Nick."

"Where's my sister?" she asked as she came into the room.

"Bathroom, she should be out in a minute," he said. "Beth said you were going to be out late."

"Hank is insufferable," she said. "I got out and took an Uber home."

"You okay?" Nick asked.

She opened the refrigerator door and got out a pitcher of tea. "I'm fine. You want some?"

He shook his head. "I'm good but Beth might need a glass." She didn't say that, but he knew after all those tears, she could be dehydrated. Joni poured two glasses and sat down at the table across from him, apparently not registering the wooden spoon on the table. A good thing. Hard to explain that.

"So want to talk about insufferable Hank?" he asked. Women did like to talk.

Joni shook her head, and he noticed for the first time her blonde hair had soft red highlights. Must run in the family. "No. He's just, you know, so male."

"Stubborn and hard headed," Nick ventured a guess.

"Exactly. I refuse to be man-splained to. I mean, I know the man is a freaking genius, but really! I'm not a slouch. Beth! Your hair!"

Nick smiled as the two sisters discussed Beth's hair and why Joni was back so early. Beth didn't seem surprised to see her.

"I invited Beth to go on a little get away the next couple of days," he told Joni. "She's agreed to go."

"But now that you and Hank aren't speaking, I really don't want to leave you alone here," Beth fretted.

Joni laughed. "Oh, you know Hank will be crawling back on his knees, probably later this evening. And if I get concerned, I can always go spend a couple nights with Ellie or Lucy. Even Jordyn would let me crash on her couch. There's no worries. I don't remember the last time you left town, Bethie."

"The day I came into town was the last day I've been out of town," Beth said. "I told Nick I was a little nervous about leaving but he said he'd bring me back if I needed to get home."

"Nick will take good care of you, right, Nick? Where are you going?"

"I will take very good care of her, and we are going over to Zephyrhills, Missouri."

"What's there?" Joni asked him, putting a plate of cookies on the table. Joni always offered him cookies. He liked that. It was a very good quality in a person. He was just a simple man.

"My brother works for a little ranch down there that rents out cabins. It will be fun to rent one out, do some fishing, some horseback riding, take some hikes and visit some of my family in the area."

"That does sound like fun. I'm almost jealous!" Joni said.

"You could come with us," Beth said suddenly.

Joni laughed. "Oh heck no, I'm no one's third wheel. I'll be fine and maybe I'll make Hank take me there for a forgive me present, if you like it and have fun."

Nick shook his head. Women. "Come on, Beth, walk me out and I'll be here to get you early in the morning. See you, Joni. Hope you and Hank make up."

"They always do," Beth told him as she got up to walk him out.

"You okay?" he asked her as they headed down the walk to his truck.

"Little nervous, but I'm going to do it, nervous or not," she said.

"There's my good girl, and maybe if you are real lucky, I'll be able to find a switch in the woods and teach you the switch dance. You might like it."

Beth giggled, then looked at him. "Tell me you aren't serious!"

"Aren't I?" he said and climbed in the truck. "See you about seven-thirty! Be ready!"

"Yes, sir!" she saluted him and he watched till her red head bobbed back inside the house with an occasional rub to her bottom, then pulled out and headed back to his cabin. On his way home, he picked up the phone and called his brother, Hunter. Hopefully, there would be a cabin, but if not, he'd rent a hotel room. Of course, they could stay with his folks, but Beth would probably feel more comfortable with a place to go and shut the door alone. Besides, he wanted the privacy with her, too. Somewhere she felt safe. Away from here.

"Hey, Hunter," he said, leaving a message. "It's Nick. give me a holler. I'm looking for a cabin for two, tomorrow and the next night. Any available?"

He hung up, knowing Hunter would call him after work. Or chores. Or whatever he called what he did out there in the big old outdoors where he often didn't receive reception.

So he dialed his mom, hoping it was her day off. "Hey, Mom," he said.

"Nicholas! I'm so glad to hear from you! How's my favorite son?"

"Wonderful, Mom, thinking of heading that way for a few days."

"That's wonderful! I'm off work right now so I'd love to have you."

"Why are you off work?" he asked, suddenly worried. His mom was only a year from retirement, she didn't need to be getting hurt now.

"Oh, just a silly little thing. Broke a couple ribs and they won't let me back to work for two more weeks. So I've been enjoying being home and working out at the farm."

"With broken ribs? Mom, I'm sure that's not what the

doctor meant when she said don't work!"

"Well, you can't sit around and do nothing, now, can you? I get enough of that at the fire station."

Nick laughed, knowing if his dad couldn't keep his mom down, no one could. "Well, I'm staying out at a cabin with Hunter, but how about feeding us tomorrow night?"

"Us?"

"Might be bringing a girl home. Mama, you treat her nice. She's shy."

His mom laughed. "Nicholas Alexander, you have never dated a shy one, don't you go lying to your mama."

"Well, she's a little different," he said. "But you'll like her."

"Of course I will. How about if we have fried chicken?"

"That would be great, I haven't had your fried chicken for quite a while."

"Anything for my favorite son," she said. "Give me a holler tomorrow and let me know what time you will be here."

"Yes, ma'am, will do. See you tomorrow."

He pulled into his drive and headed down to his cabin. It would be great to get away for a few days, see his family, do some fishing, ride a horse, he'd see if there was something Beth wanted to do, too. Spelunk or hike, whatever. He'd try and show her a good time. See if he could get that little worry line between her brows to disappear for a few days. It would be good to have her with him so he didn't have that niggling little worry about her safety constantly. When and how had she gotten so important to him? He guessed there was no reason to analyze it, the fact was, she had wormed her way into his heart, and he could only hope he did the same to hers. He had no intention of overthinking it, he just wanted a weekend away with her and see how she reacted to his family. He hoped they liked her and they would, but really it didn't matter. He liked her. The mystery of his little non mouse intrigued him.

Chapter 5

Beth settled into the front seat of his truck, after he'd stashed her bag in the back. After he left last night, she and Joni had made a quick mall run and she'd bought some jeans that actually fit as well as a couple pair of shorts and a semi modest bathing suit just in case there was a hot tub somewhere. Then a few shirts had caught their eye and she ended up spending a lot more than she'd thought, but it felt so good to wear clothes that fit again. She was tired of hiding in more ways than one. No matter what, she was taking her old life back. Slowly, but she was going to do it.

She felt ready for anything in her new outfit of jeans, a pull over bright yellow shirt, and her ball cap covered in sequins and rhinestones. She hadn't worn anything sparkly in years. It felt good. Her signature on the pitcher's mound was her sparkly baseball cap. Her lucky charm and she hadn't worn it since she moved. It was time it saw the light of day again. Hopefully it would bring her good luck this week, which, basically only meant a little bit of stress free time with him.

"So, what's your cap mean? I'm off this weekend, I don't want to hear any sirens," Nick asked her.

Beth laughed. "Name of my old ball team. We were The Sirens. In Greek mythology, sirens were women who were very beautiful and very dangerous."

"Well, you have the beautiful down, how dangerous are you?"

Beth felt herself blush. Thing about her red hair, the blush felt much more noticeable. She hoped it wasn't. "On the mound, pretty darn dangerous," she said.

"Good to know. Tell me when you need a pit stop, we have over a four hour drive ahead of us."

"I will," she said. "Thanks, that was thoughtful."

"This is our weekend, not just mine," he said. "Both of us are to have a good time. Well, except we might cover a few uncomfortable topics." He looked her way and smiled and she looked back warily. What did he mean by that?

"Like what?" she said. "You know more about me than most people."

"Do I?"

"Don't you?"

Nick laughed and said, "Think about what kind of food you want for lunch and we will find a good place along the way, okay?"

"So, what are we doing this weekend?" she asked, scrolling on her phone to find someplace good to eat in the next couple hundred miles.

"First of all, we are enjoying the ride and having a great lunch. Then if you want, we are going to stop and take a tour of Meramec Caverns before we get to–"

"Are you serious?" Beth interrupted, almost bouncing in her seat. "I've always wanted to do that!"

"I'm serious," he said, and gave her a look she didn't understand. "We should be out of there by three, at my folks' by five or so where Mom's making dinner, then will check in to our little getaway place after. Tomorrow, we have a bunch of options but can decide either tonight or tomorrow."

"I'm meeting your mom tonight? You didn't tell me that! I'm not wearing meeting the mom clothes!"

"Meeting the mom clothes? When Mom isn't at work, she lives in jeans and shirts. What you have on is the least of your worries."

Beth took a deep breath. "So what is the worst of my worries?"

"Keeping me from beating your butt again."

He said it so matter of factly she couldn't help but giggle. "Yes. I worry about that so much."

"Good. That is my goal," he said.

"Well, I might be a little more worried about meeting your mom. And your dad, I assume. Any of your brothers going to be there?"

He shrugged. "I don't know. Depends on their work schedules."

"So tell me about them. Just in case?" Beth didn't care about meeting his family, really. The old Beth could rise to the occasion and meet and greet and often, mostly, charm almost everyone. The people who liked the old Beth outweighed those who didn't. She hoped, but she knew the new Beth was a good combination of the outgoing, overly confident person she was and the hermit she had been. Had she met in a happy middle? Perhaps she was still working on it. She'd find out tonight, more than likely. This would be her first group meet. But right now, she had the cavern to look forward to exploring. Oh, and information on his brothers.

"Dax is the oldest. His name is Ryan Daxton but we call him Dax. He's a firefighter like Mom and Dad and works with them. He has a house in town, and just got divorced. He has the only grandkid, a little girl named Addie who is four and a little doll. She's with her mom most of the time."

"If she's got your genes, I bet she's gorgeous," Beth said, trying to imagine a small female version of Nick. Well, Nick's brother who might look nothing like Nick. She and her sisters didn't look alike, after all.

He ignored that. "Then there is Sam who is a mechanic. Then me, Caleb and I'm not sure what Caleb is doing now, but he likes his inside jobs, as opposed to the rest of us, and Hunter. Hunter is the youngest and works out on the ranch. That's where we will be staying tonight."

"With him?" Beth asked, her head spinning a little and really hoping they all weren't showing up for supper or that she'd be sharing a cabin with Hunter.

"No, we get our own little place. We aren't sharing with any of my brothers. I don't share. Ever."

Beth smiled. "Okay. That sounds good to me."

"You are remarkably cool and collected for such a basket case," he said.

"Excuse me! I am not a basket case! I am rightfully cautious and extremely conservative" She tried to sound as indignant as she could. Really, she often could be classified as a basket case.

"If you say so," Nick said and turned on the blinker. "Rest stop, then lunch in an hour, wherever you picked."

Beth smiled. This would be a good weekend. This guy she was with was going to make it one.

Six hours later they pulled into his parents' driveway. There were a handful of cars already lined up in the long, double wide drive. "Looks like we might be late," she worried.

"Nah, we're the stars of the show," he said. "I've not brought a girl home in ages. They can't wait to meet you."

"Umm, what?"

"Yeah, I didn't date in high school, and then at college,

well, we were too busy to come home often. Though now and then I brought someone here but usually my brothers ran them off. I'm assuming they've grown up enough not to do that. But then I moved. So they're probably all really curious about you."

Beth grabbed his hand when he opened the car door. "You won't tell them about, well, you know?"

Nick shook his head. "That's not my story to tell. I won't say anything, ever, you aren't comfortable with."

"Well, but for 'get over my lap right now, young lady' you mean?"

"Yeah, that's what I meant. Come on. Meet the family."

Beth's head spun within minutes. There were his parents, who didn't seem near retirement age to her. His mom, who insisted she call her Molly, had a head full of thick dark hair, that must be where Nick and his brothers got theirs. His dad, Ryan, was quiet and more reserved than outgoing Molly, but even after a lot of years and five kids, his eyes still followed Molly around the room. He had a head full of salt and pepper hair and she wondered if he was much older than Molly.

Three of his brothers were there, the oldest Dax, was at work. But Sam, Caleb and Hunter were more than enough for her to get confused. So many dark headed handsome males! The old her would have Scarlett O'Hara at the barbeque all over them.

However, they were all funny, loud and she really enjoyed seeing Nick relax and be just as goofy and playful as they were. It was a side of him she didn't see often, but vowed to herself to try and bring it out more. When had her life gotten so somber? That wasn't her.

"Let me help," she said, following Molly into the kitchen after she announced she was checking on the food.

"It's all done," she told her, "but for a quick stir of the

gravy if you want to grab the spoon. Hope you like fried chicken."

"Love it," Beth said.

"So how did you and Nick meet?" she asked, pulling a platter out of the oven.

"My sister knocked the grill over and set the lawn on fire," Beth said. "Nick came to the rescue."

"That's a fun story to tell the grandkids," Molly said. "No pressure!"

"We haven't been dating that long," Beth protested, and saw the smile on Molly's face.

"If I didn't give the boys grief about grandkids, they would be disappointed. I have one granddaughter but don't get to see her nearly enough."

"I'm sorry about that," Beth said.

"What are you apologizing to my mother for?" Nick came in and took the gravy spoon from her hand.

"Addie," his mom said. "I was just wishing I could see her more."

"We all do," Nick agreed. "Hopefully things will settle down there soon." He reached up in the cabinet and grabbed a gravy boat while Beth stepped back. "The salad is in the fridge," he told Beth. "Grab the tongs from that drawer over there."

He was a natural in the kitchen, even though he kept telling her he couldn't cook, and between the three of them, they had the food on the table in just a few minutes. "We set the table, which means, they clear," he told Beth.

"Good system," she said, as he patted the chair beside him. Hard and wooden and her bottom was still a little tender from last night but no way was she letting him know it. She sat down and didn't even wince once.

"So what do you see in this lunk?" one of the brothers asked her.

"You mean hunk, I assume," Nick said to the moans of his brothers.

"Well, his charm and good looks and he told me he's secretly a billionaire with a red room and a helicopter, and I'm just all shallow like that," Beth said.

The brother, Caleb, maybe, nodded sagely. "Yeah, that one gets the pretty girls every time."

"Hey, if a line works," Nick said. "Pass the salt please." One of his brother's lobbed it across the table and Beth reached out and deftly caught it before it arrived. It had been an automatic grab and she blushed as the brothers hooted and teased Nick. She hadn't meant to do that.

"Sorry," she whispered to Nick, handing him the salt shaker.

He laughed. "You saved me from a fumble."

"I think fumble is football, not a salt shaker," she said.

"Or just Nick's life." She heard as she tried to hide. What had she done? Would he be upset?

Nick laughed again, apparently giving each other a hard time was what brothers did and she suddenly felt glad she grew up with sisters, even though she always wanted a brother. Maybe they were overrated.

A bit later, feeling full, she stayed sitting, a little uncomfortably, due to both her sore bottom and feeling as if she should help while the other men cleared the table, then brought in two pies. There was no way she could eat pie. She was too full, and yet, there was a piece of the most gorgeous lemon meringue in front of her. It rivaled Jordyn's who made the best pie she ever had, just about as good as her grandmother's whose was only better by virtue of love.

She took a few very wonderful bites then slid her plate over to Nick to finish. No one noticed and she sat quietly and watched them. Suddenly, she felt exhausted and hoped they would be able to leave soon. Everyone was wonderful, but she'd had a really long day on top of a stressful week. She bit her lip to stifle a yawn, but noticed that Nick looked sharply at her.

"Well, this was wonderful, but we need to go. Mom, I'll give you a call tomorrow. I'd really like to show Beth the farm. You going to be out there?"

"Most of the day," she said, cheerfully. "Just let us know, but if you get busy, it will be here next time."

"Thanks, Mom. Love you," he said. "See you soon, Dad. As for you guys" – Nick took Beth's hand and led her toward the door – "just eat your hearts out." Beth blushed and let him lead her outside.

They pulled up in front of the cabin and Beth looked around tiredly. After a good night's sleep, she'd be excited to look around this ranch or farm or whatever it was. Right now, she wanted a quick shower and to go to bed. Would there be two beds? She didn't care, she didn't think anyway. Trusting Nick was an instinct she couldn't overcome. He'd take care of her, no matter what. She knew that intellectually, but hoped she would be able to cope in real life. She might trust him but her nerves still jangled.

They walked into the small cozy cabin that rather resembled his at home. It seemed to be a small almost studio, with the bed, the one bed, in front of the fireplace and a tiny kitchenette in the corner, and what she hoped was a bathroom door. "Dibs on the bathroom," she said as they carried in their bags. Yes, it was the bathroom, she found out when she opened it. Dropping her overnight bag on the counter, she turned the shower on and did a quick wash, then slipped on her oversized ball jersey and a clean pair of panties, and brushed her teeth. She did feel a little more refreshed but still ready for bed. Quickly, she hung up her towel, and cleaned the sink, then went out where Nick had started a fire and her heart pounded. She was actually going to sleep in the bed with him. In front of the fire. The romantic fire.

"Aww, my little ball player," he said, turning from where he knelt in front of the fire, feeding it logs. "I know it's a little warm, but we can turn the ceiling fan on. I thought you might want to look at the fire."

"I do," she said and tried to stop her teeth from chattering with sudden nerves. "Bathroom is all yours," she managed.

He grabbed his bag and headed that direction while she eyed the fire and the bed. This was Nick. She was safe. There was nothing to worry about. Going into the small kitchen, she grabbed a water bottle from the fridge and took a sip, noticing her fingers were shaking. Did he expect her to, well, did she want to? Yeah, she did, but she wasn't sure she could. She had to tell him. Talk to him. Could she? She didn't know that either. Why hadn't she thought of this before they left? What should she do? Go to bed and pretend she was asleep?

No, that would be a lie. She was never lying to Nick. She stood in front of the fire, as if frozen, clutching her drink like a lifeline.

He came out of the bathroom, toweling his hair, wearing another towel slung around his hips in the way only men could wear them. The man was fine, more than fine, and she felt terrified.

"I figured you'd already be asleep," he said.

She relaxed a little. Okay, maybe he just hadn't assumed. The relief rushed through her.

"I almost am," she said. "But well, Nick?"

She just wanted him to know what she needed and couldn't deal with, and wanted and was afraid of, yet desired. It was too much to ask of one male. She knew that. Not being stupid didn't stop her from wanting it though. Or being afraid to tell him.

He walked to her. "What, little Damsel?"

"I'm scared."

"You're with me. There is nothing to be afraid of. Come on, let's just go to bed and be close. Nothing else but talking and looking at the fire." He took her hand and she followed him to the very cozy looking bed. She really wanted to be in bed. She would love him to hold her. But he needed to know. However, he took control as he always did, in a way that made her feel safe.

Peeling back the covers, he plumped a pillow and gently but firmly sat her down then turned her around, so she was against the pillow and looking at the fire. Then he covered her up and kissed her forehead.

Going to the other side of the bed, he climbed in and cuddled next to her while she stiffened, reminding herself this was Nick. He was a good guy. She was safe. And yet. "I'm scared," she whispered.

"What are you afraid of?" he asked as he stroked her shoulders, then pulled her closer so she laid her head on his chest. Oh, yeah, she liked this. But, she tried to catch her breath, or slow it down and couldn't. Yet, she needed to talk to him. Or she could just drift off to sleep and put it off. There. She managed a deep calming breath.

"You feel good," he said. "I like your little red head on me."

"Umm…" she murmured, snuggling in. Him. He was safe. He would understand she couldn't. "You feel good, too. But, Nick?"

"Tell me, baby, what is it?"

"I'm scared."

"I know that. Why? Yes, I will paddle you when you need it, but I will only do the best for you. I will never scare you or be mean to you. You know that, right?"

She nodded her head. Yeah, he spanked her but she wasn't afraid of him. She just needed to talk to him.

"I do. But, Nick–" She took a deep breath. "The last time I did something, I didn't want to." She felt him stiffen under her, then relax, but there was a pause as if he were collecting himself.

"The next time you do, you will want to. It won't be tonight though. I promise. Just cuddle up, and be close but go to sleep knowing you are safe here with me."

Somehow, she just trusted him. He would do nothing to her she didn't want. Well, except spank her, but, really, she could deal with that, and for some reason even that made her feel safe and cared for. Weird, but true. Even if she didn't like it.

It took a few minutes for her to get comfortable, but once she did, she sighed in contentment and fell asleep. Her last thought was that she hoped she didn't drool on him in her sleep.

Beth swung down off her horse and couldn't stop smiling. "That was the best time," she told Nick. "I haven't been on a horse in years. Thank you!"

"I had a good time, too," he told her. "Let's get these guys unsaddled and brushed down."

"Yes!" Beth took Silver's reins, and followed Nick toward the barn. "Thank you," she told her horse. "You don't know what today meant to me." The horse snuffled in her ear, making her giggle. "I'm glad you had a good time, too."

Nick laughed as they walked inside the huge barn, which smelled of hay and horses. She loved that smell, and his laugh. Leading their horses to their stalls, they unsaddled them and took their bridles off. He tossed her a large curry comb and they both went to work brushing their horses down. "Do you ride often?" she asked him.

"Not anymore. My brothers and I grew up riding on our grandpa's farm, though. He always had a couple horses. I think that's where Caleb got his love for them. He works here but also works at the farm that Mom and Dad are moving to. I'm sure he hopes to inherit it one day."

"Tell me about the farm," she asked him.

"We can go look at it if you want," he said. "My folks are fixing it up and planning to move there as soon as Mom retires next year."

"I like your mom," she said. "Your dad is quiet, but he seems nice."

Nick smiled. "Yeah, he is nice. One day I want a marriage like they have.

"Happy one?" she asked.

"Yeah. Happy."

"Most people want that," she said. "You just never know people though. They aren't always what they act like in the beginning. They change. Or just flat out lie."

"Is that what Eli did? " he asked from behind the horse.

It was easier to talk to him from behind a horse. "No. I changed when I found out what he was doing. Then he reacted to what I was doing."

"So him beating you up and raping you and putting you in the hospital is your fault?"

He was lucky he was behind the horse, and couldn't see her, because her tears welled up and rolled down her cheeks. Yeah, sometimes, too often, even despite therapy, she did feel that way. Like it was all her fault and she should have been able to stop it. Not done what she did. Why had she done that? She'd ruined his life. All he'd done was cheat on his wife but she ruined his life. What would she do if someone ruined hers, or her sisters'? She didn't know. She deserved something. Maybe not what happened, but something.

She didn't answer him. He'd just scold her for saying yes and she wasn't going to lie, so there was that.

"There you go, Silver. All gorgeous and ready for a treat." She wiped her eyes and walked out from the side of the horse to give her an apple from the basket by the stall. She slipped out and fastened the lock. "I need a shower," she said.

"Me, too," he said, coming out of his stall. "Let's go do that, get some food and maybe go for a walk by the lake?"

"Sounds wonderful," she said. Suck it up, she told herself. Fake it till you make it. Be cheerful. It is his holiday, after all. He didn't need all this deep introspection and angst on his weekend away with his family. "Is Hunter joining us for dinner?"

"No, why?"

She shrugged. "I just thought since he lived here, well…"

"Did you want him to join us? I can call him." Nick looked at her.

Beth shook her head. "Nope. I just want to be with you."

"Good girl," he said and made her smile. What was with that phrase? "We are going to meet everyone who isn't working tomorrow for brunch at Mom's favorite place, though, if that works for you. Then maybe go out to the farm. We will head home by four or so and be home before midnight."

She nodded again. Tomorrow. That meant there was a whole entire night to get through still. Suddenly, all she wanted was to be in her little office with all the doors locked.

Standing in the shower, later, she let the tears flow. Just a little bit of culture shock, she told herself. And she was a little overwhelmed right now. He had such a happy, close family. What had that been like? Growing up, it was just her mom and sisters most of their lives. Their mom was gone at work much more than she was home. Joni was off with her friends as often as she could be, and Sydney was always locked in her room studying. She always had her ball teams, though, and later in high school, somehow became one of the popular kids. Then, her world crashed and now she basically was alone, without even a ball team to rely on for support or socialization.

Shutting off the water, she got dressed in soft white pants and a light blue blouse, perfect for whatever he wanted to do, and left to put her make up on out in the big room, to let him have the bathroom. See how thoughtful she was?

He showered more quickly than she did, she noticed as he came out a few minutes later, toweling his head.

"What are you doing?" he asked.

"Putting makeup on," she said.

"Why?"

Beth giggled. Okay, that was funny. "Even an old barn looks better with a fresh coat of paint," she told him.

"What barn? I think you are gorgeous."

"Thank you, but I'm sure it's the paint."

"Take it off," he said and continued toweling his hair dry as if he weren't half-naked making ridiculous statements.

"Take it off?" She stroked more mascara on her eye lashes. "What are you talking about?"

"I like you without all the goop on your face. It feels like a mask. I don't want you hiding from me."

"It isn't a mask. It's makeup."

"What is makeup supposed to do?"

"Make me look better and feel better," she said, capping the mascara tube, and picking up the lip gloss.

"Does it make you feel better?"

She shrugged. She never really thought about it. "I guess, maybe?"

"Why?" He opened his suitcase on the bed and got out a shirt. She watched him put it on. Abs like that should not be covered, in her opinion. Maybe he felt the same way about makeup.

"How about I leave it on for dinner, then take it off?" she compromised.

"I'd prefer you take it off now, but I'll accept that," he said. She put her makeup away and he grabbed her hand. "I think you are just beautiful, you know. There is no reason to hide your face, or your hair, or that slamming hot body anymore. You are safe with me, and here."

Oh. That was the issue. The hiding, not the makeup. With her free hand, she saluted him and gave him a saucy smile. "Yes, sir! Let's go eat. Horseback riding makes me hungry."

"I know the best little steakhouse," he said, grabbing his keys and wallet. "Let's go."

Beth inhaled deeply as they walked out. "Isn't it funny how Missouri air smells different than Illinois air? And I figured out your accent."

"I don't have an accent," he said, opening the truck door and smacking her ass as she climbed in. Would she ever get tired of that? It was as if he were staking a claim on her. Nothing wrong with that.

"Yeah, it is really subtle but it's there. Your brothers have it, too. Your dad has it more. Where is he from?"

"Texas," he said. "Moved up here after he met Mom."

"That's it," she said, almost triumphantly. "Texas twang!"

Nick snorted. "I don't have a twang!"

She nodded and wagged her finger in his face. "Don't you argue with me, Nick Kinkirk! I know a twang when I hear a twang!"

"Yes, ma'am," he said, and laid on the accent thick. "I do understand that, yes I do."

Beth giggled, feeling better. She was on a break. Not worrying or looking over her shoulder was on her agenda, nothing more than that, but enjoying time getting to know Nick.

She could smell the smoke from the grill and hot yeasty rolls as they pulled into the parking lot. Inhaling deeply, she could feel her stomach rumble. Food! It seemed like forever ago they'd shared a little picnic on the trail ride. He grabbed her hand as they walked toward the door.

Inside, it was loud and smelled so good, she wondered if she could get full off the smell alone.

He ordered them both steak, baked potatoes and corn on the cob, with frosty mugs of beer to wash it down.

"Why did you ever leave here?" she asked him. "I don't know if I could have."

"They have a steakhouse in Clearwater," he said.

"That isn't what I meant," she said, picking up her fork to eat her salad. "Your family is all here, and you grew up here, wasn't it hard to leave?"

Nick shook his head. "No, I was glad to go. I knew here, I'd always be Ryan and Molly's kid, and Dax's baby brother. In Clearwater, I'm me."

She nodded. She understood that. "So there was no big blow up or anything?"

He put some extra dressing on his salad. "Well, sure, we had the usual fights and things when I was a kid, but that's normal. I just decided one day, I wanted to see more, see what was outside of our little town and family. I started applying out of state and had a couple offers. Clearwater offered everything I was wanting."

"Was your family upset when you moved?" she asked.

He shrugged. "I was the first one who did, but no one seemed unduly upset about it. Mom thinks I'll move back before too long. How about you? Did it bother your mom when all three of you moved?"

Beth shook her head. "Sydney said she probably didn't even notice for a month or two."

Nick looked at her, oddly. "She didn't know?"

Beth laughed. "Oh sure, she knew, but she also knew why. She's just busy and has a very important, very demanding job."

He nodded. "I know. With two firefighter parents, we were alone a lot, too. Our grandma and grandpa stepped in a lot, though. We never felt like we were alone."

"I imagine anyone with an ounce of common sense wouldn't leave five boys home alone for long," she said.

"Hey, we were perfect angels, all the time. That's my story and I'm sticking to it, no matter what you hear."

Beth smiled and relaxed, vowing to just enjoy the rest of the evening and not worry about anything for a change. It would be remarkable if she could do that, but she was going to try.

"I like your hair," he told her. "It's getting longer."

"I miss my long hair," she confessed. "I can't wait for it to grow out again."

"How long was it?" he asked.

"Down to my waist," she said. Something she never told anyone. "He hacked about half of it off with scissors during a time I was half conscious. They couldn't find any hair, so they assume he took it with him."

"Why?"

She shook her head. "He never said. They thought he was obsessed with me. I know better. He was mad. He probably burned it or turned it into a voodoo doll or something."

Nick stabbed at his last piece of potato and Beth was glad it wasn't her. He didn't seem happy.

"The man has issues," he finally said.

Beth shrugged. "We all do. I guess most of us don't know what we will or won't do in dramatic situations."

"Can I interest you in a dessert?" the waitress asked.

Beth shook her head, and Nick said, "Just the check please."

"I'm ready to walk off dinner and the horse soreness," she told him.

"Hmmm, I think I can arrange that," he said.

"Good."

They got out of the truck at a walking path near the small lake on the ranch. "The moon is gorgeous," she said. "But you are going to have to watch for werewolves."

"Werewolves? Do they come out in a full moon?"

"Pretty sure they do," she said. "We will have to keep an eye out."

Between the full moon and the solar lights marking the path, they had no problem following it. "Shh!" she whispered. "What was that?"

"What was what?"

"I think I heard a werewolf!"

"Need me to save you?" he asked.

"Maybe I should save you! I'm not the one with the beard. They will think you are one of them!" She looked around and saw a small path into the woods, off the main path. "Hurry!" She darted off into the woods, with him hot on her heels.

"Beth! Watch out! There might be traps!" he called out.

Giggling, she found a small opening in the woods and ran in there, as he stormed past her, then stopped and turned around. Holding her breath, she waited to see if he would find her.

She heard nothing for a very long silent minute, then just as she was thinking of finding him, or calling out, she felt a hand on her neck and shrieked loudly.

"Hey, little Red, the big bad wolf has you under his control now," he whispered in her ear. "And you know what big bad wolves want?"

"My picnic basket?" She relaxed against him.

"Nope, the wolf is full of supper. Wolf wants a kiss and then to punish the little girl who ran away from him," he said.

"Maybe she doesn't need punished," she said, softly.

"That isn't her call now, is it?" he said, nibbling on her neck while she shivered. "You can't let a little one get away with bad behavior. It only encourages it. Nope, I'm pretty sure a spanking is in order."

Beth stifled her giggle. "No! Not that! Anything but that!"

"Sorry, that's what it has to be," he said and relaxed his grasp enough for her to jerk away and take a few running steps. He grabbed her and half carried her to a tall stump. "And trying to dodge out of it! For shame!"

He sat down on the stump and pulled her over his lap. Her hands sunk into the deep mulch and she hoped there were no critters in there.

"No! No! I'll be good! I promise! Please Mr. Wolf! Don't spank me!"

"Darn right you will be good!" he said, and smacked her bottom a few times while she obligingly squealed for him and tried to stop the giggles. "There are werewolves in the forest but I'm the baddest wolf of them all."

"Nah, you're just a baby wolf," she teased. "Barely able to cope out in the big bad forest."

"What did you just say?" he asked while peppering light spanks all over her bottom, making it tingle wonderfully.

"I said you spank like a girl!" she said, then shrieked delightedly as he smacked her harder.

"And you think that's an insult?" he said.

"Pretty sure little boys think it is! Ow!" she bit back a giggle again.

"Little boys! What happened to big bad wolf?" He smacked her several more times and she felt her bottom warm up and begin to sting and decided this was much better than a cathartic crying spanking. This one was rather, well, hot.

"I don't know! I think he, *ow*! He must have run away and left you here instead. Ow! Ow!" She wiggled against him and squirmed hard, just to hear him moan.

"Left me here instead? I am the bad wolf, little Red, and don't you forget it!" She giggled and kicked her legs but didn't dare move her hands. Last thing she wanted was leaves in her hair.

"Ouch! I mean, ohh, that didn't hurt," she said and wiggled some more, just to feel his reaction.

"I'm sorry. The bad wolf will try to do better." He peppered her bottom with sharp stinging spanks that didn't do much more than turn her on even more. She hadn't felt that in a very long time and relished it. However, she obligingly kicked and squealed and protested. This was much different from the other spankings. This kind of spanking she could enjoy.

Before she was even ready, he seemed to be done, standing up and pulling her up with him.

Standing her up in front of him, he tipped her head up and looked into her eyes. "Are you sorry?"

"Sorry that you're not really the big bad wolf? Yup." Nick leaned down, and kissed her softly, then a little harder, then gave a low deep growl.

"We will just see about that," he said, and smacked her already warm bottom while she yelped.

"Ouch! I'm sorry. You are the baddest wolf in the forest."

"I thought you'd see it my way," he said, almost too smugly while she snickered.

"Oh, I do, Sir, I really really do!"

"Come on. Let's go back to the cabin."

She couldn't wait to get back to the cabin with him. It was time.

Chapter 6

It had been over four months since she found out Eli was in town. Other than the first time she'd found the olives in the refrigerator, and that one time she knew she'd seen him in the parking lot at the Running Water when her mom was in town, he'd not been around as far as she knew. He and Miranda had been seen out and about by her, Joni and some of Joni's friends. She couldn't count those, though, as him coming around her. So far he hadn't approached her, or her sister and while she hated he was in town, she had become accustomed to the fact that he was. She even started to relax a little when she was out.

If he wanted to get in, to see her, to do something, he would have by now, right? Still, she and Joni were still taking precautions and being safe. It was getting very tiresome though, even in a 'this is now normal' kind of way. Sometimes she almost wished he would do something, and get it over with so the anxiety wasn't always simmering. Not that she really wanted to be in the hospital for days again though. The very last thing she wanted was for Joni to get caught in the crosshairs. That scared her more than actually getting hurt herself again.

She'd thought a time or two or a hundred about going over to confront him, but the thought of Nick finding out deterred her. Whether the idea of disappointing him or the idea of the paddling she'd get if she did, yeah, she wasn't risking either one of those things. Him being upset or her standing for a week, neither interested her. Plus there was that pesky legal protection order. He was to stay away from her, but she had to stay away from him, too. If Nick had taught her anything, it was to obey the rules or pay the consequences. His consequences or the law's, neither were fun, or worth it. Probably.

"Hey, Joni," she said. "I'm ready if you are!"

Joni looked up from papers she was grading, and scowled. "Is it time? Sorry, I'm running a bit late. Can you wait an hour?"

"Seriously?" Disappointment shot through her.

"No, silly! I'm ready. Let's go pick up your car!" She put the papers down on the table and laughed. "I bet you are so excited!"

Beth laughed. This had been a long time coming. She couldn't wait to get her car and be able to go at her whim. Borrowing Joni's had gotten old for both of them, though Joni never complained.

But now, a new car would be parked in their driveway tonight. Her new car that she could use to do whatever whenever. Including going to Nick's little cabin if she chose to go there.

It didn't take long to do the paperwork at the dealership, they'd even put new plates on it for her, it sparkled from cleanliness, and it had that new car smell. If she kept the windows rolled up, would it linger for a while? She hoped so. But then, she wanted to go for a drive around the lake and knew it would smell amazing out there. Pointing her shiny silver car toward the lake, she started driving. She'd heard there was going to be a new bed and breakfast opening out there soon, and wanted to go look at it, just to be nosy. Plus, sadly, she hadn't driven around the lake since she moved to town.

Things had changed a lot. Some of it was her hair. Some of Joni's friends didn't even recognize her when they saw her. Her attitude had changed, too, she knew. Even though Eli was still around town, and she got glimpses of him now and again, which never failed to shake her up and the thrill of nerves never lessened, she wasn't looking around every corner anymore. She knew she couldn't let her guard down, but felt a little more relaxed.

Why was he here? What did he want and if it was her, he certainly was playing a long game. If it wasn't her, why was he here of all places in the entire world to be and live in? Too much of a coincidence and while she did believe in coincidence, she didn't believe in this one. But she put him out of her head as she got closer to the gorgeous lake. The leaves had exploded into their brilliant early fall foliage colors making her smile as she drank in their beauty. She smiled in her car, her own car, she reminded herself. Another change in her life. She noticed a small sign, with an arrow announcing, "Willow's Inn". That had to be it. Were they open already? Or just being proactive for the worker people? She hadn't seen any announcements, but she might have missed it. The paved road wandered lazily around the lake and she drank in the view.

There it was. Clearly not open yet. There were about ten trucks parked in front of it, and the sounds of power tools she could hear even through her rolled up windows. Slowing down, she did the gawker thing and watched people walk around the huge old house, painters and people working on windows and she wasn't sure what all else. Was it technically a mansion? She didn't know. But it was big, and interesting looking, many turrets and dormers, a huge wide front porch that overlooked the lake. It looked as if it might be a soft sea blue when it was done being painted.

She found a small place about half a mile up the road, and pulled in to turn around and drive back by on her way home. They would probably have an open house when they opened and when they did, she'd come out and explore, she decided. Why not?

As she drove by again, among all the men in hard hats and boots, she saw Miranda striding by in her stilettos and tight skirt. Of course. Shaking her head, wondering, as always, how she walked in those, she caught her breath and instinctively hit the brake.

Trailing behind Miranda was Eli. Shivering she felt herself begin to sweat and she gripped the steering wheel tightly, forcing her eyes to the road and her foot to the gas. Home. Just go home, she told herself taking a slow deep breath. She was fine. No one knew her car and she had her sunglasses hiding her eyes.

Cautiously, she made sure to drive as carefully as she could right at the speed limit. Suddenly the bright fall day seemed a little ominous. She had her new car, she could go home, pack a bag and move. Maybe to Nick's hometown. Maybe back to Chicago. Maybe some island in the middle of nowhere.

Did she want to leave Clearwater? Not really. She'd only just now started to explore and meet people and enjoy it. Did she want to keep running into Eli, ruining her day and making her miserable? No to that, too. He needed to move. Why was he here? It all kept coming back to that. How could she find out? There was Miranda obviously. No one talked to Miranda on purpose though. The last time she'd tried to talk to her, to warn her, had not gone well. There was nothing that made her think Miranda would want to talk to her, or even less, to share intimate details about the man she was dating.

Was that his long game? Just to move here and make her miserable knowing he was around? Probably. That made as much sense as anything else. Well, she wasn't going to be miserable or afraid. That would show him. He had too much power over her brain and she didn't like that either. Her brain was on triple overload and wouldn't shut or slow down. All she could think of was why and options. Why was he doing this and what were her options and there seemed to be a million different ways to think about both.

Sighing, she pointed her shiny new car toward home and safety and away from him. She wished her hunky fireman was around, but he wasn't. He was working, and in the middle of a thirty-six-hour-long shift, covering for someone. The upside to that, though was he would be getting an extra day or two off and promised they would do something fun. Their relationship was much more her style now, more of her old self, but a little more toned down, or grown up. She no longer acted out for attention. There was very little drama and anytime things began to escalate, he solved the problem quickly and decisively. Sometimes just by giving her a look, one she thought of as 'The Look', and that usually quelled her emotions. Then, of course, his favorite, putting her over his knee.

Shaking her head, she half smiled, feeling better already. Maybe that was why the new her was so much calmer and less excitable than the old her. Meeting the board of education had an effect, that was for sure. Oddly, while she did fear the pain of a spanking, she did not fear him or resent him for doing it. In fact, sometimes she seemed to crave it in some weird spot in her brain or body, and he often picked up on that. How? She didn't know that either. The ways of the male mind were very mysterious.

Getting home, she parked next to Joni's car, glad they had a wide driveway. Although it would be safe, she didn't want to park her new baby in the street. It – she – needed cared for and coddled. Maybe she should name it? Why not? What did one name a car besides Sally, which she felt was way over-done? Something to think about while she worked.

Heading into the house, she noted Joni wasn't home, even though her car was. Probably over at Hank's house next door. They were doing the on again stage. The man really needed to grow a backbone. Why he let her get away with her antics, baffled her. The mysterious male mind again. Every time she'd start an argument or throw a fit, or jump out of the car while ten miles from home, he'd just let her and come crawling back to apologize. Beth could never figure for what, but then she realized that, before, she had done the same thing to men and they had reacted the same way. Let her throw her fits and weight around and then bring her presents and worm their way back in her life. She'd loved it and lapped it up. The few times Hank had stood up to her, like when he insisted they get a new barbeque a while back, Joni seemed happier. Why didn't he know that or make the connection? Of course, none of the men she'd gone out with had either.

Till Nick. She didn't know if it was the way Nick handled himself, situations, or her, or that she was different now. What would the old Beth have done if he'd threatened her with a spanking, and then followed through? Dared them to, till they backed down probably. Not Nick. He just calmly took control and followed through.

She sat down at her computer and turned it on, thinking. If she felt as if she were spiraling, he knew it and knew if she needed a hug or a spanking. How? Why? The other big ques-tion. What was she to him? He seemed to like her well enough, and sometimes way more than enough, but who did he like? The Damsel in distress? What would happen when she no longer was in distress? Surely this couldn't drag on much longer.

Quickly, she typed Eli's name and Clearwater into the

computer, easily finding his new address and employment. Her fancy insurance company software shouldn't be used for this, but oh well. It wasn't like they'd really care. She didn't see it as an invasion of privacy. He'd done much worse to her. And she'd done much worse to him, she reminded herself. So what were a couple little computer clicks?

She stared at the screen. He lived in the newest apartment complex on the edge of town, more than a few miles from her. He worked for a construction company. She half wondered if it was the one Ben, Jordyn's fiancé, ran. She knew his business had exploded since he moved to town, and had been doing side jobs like her bathroom. Now, he had a dozen or so employees and could be seen hard at work all over town. She didn't even know Eli knew how to be a carpenter. He was keyboard clicking when they were together, working for his father-in-law, though she didn't know that at the time.

She sighed. It looked like he was here in town for a while if not to stay. Why, why, why? It was making her crazy. She didn't want to live as if the shoe was always going to drop. What other choice did she have? He'd come to town, let her know he could get to her anytime and then just let her stew. What kind of sick game was that?

Beth shook her head, and clicked off the program, then opened her game folder. She needed to wreck a car or two, work off some mental energy.

"You up for an inspection today?"

Nick looked up from the pot of chili he'd stuck the ladle into. He didn't know who made it but it sure looked good. Even if it was nine in the morning.

"Sure," he said, easily. "Just tell me where, what and when." He didn't mind getting out of the firehouse and putting some homeowner's mind at ease or make sure a business would be customer safe.

An hour later, his belly full of chili, he was heading to the lake. There was a new BnB out there and he had the privilege of inspecting the recently installed fire and carbon monoxide alarms. Nick wasn't sure how he got that privilege, but he was excited. It had been a very long boring couple of days. Very few calls, no fires which, while good things, made the days long and full of cleaning. Getting away a while would be a great change of pace.

His place was the other way, and he didn't go this route very often. He should make an effort to do it more, he decided. It was gorgeous out here. Fall was one of his four favorite seasons. There was something to like about every one of them.

Nick knew where the BnB was located, he'd driven out there once a while back, just to look at it, as he suspected many of the people in town did. The old house had sat empty for years and it was good to both have a new business in town and one less empty house.

He got out and looked around at the bustling workers, and made his way to the door. Miranda met him, instead of the owner.

"Hello, Miranda," he said, taking off his helmet he'd been wearing. "How's the work coming along?"

"It's getting there, " she said. "I assume you are the inspector."

"Yes, ma'am," he said. "Nick Kinkirk."

"Okay, I'll leave you to it," she said. "You know what you are doing, right?"

"Yes, ma'am," he said, getting out his kit.

"Then, do your job," she said brusquely and turned away. He watched her walk away with a half-smile. She had a reputation and lived up to it. His hand itched, but he firmly put the thought of teaching her a few manners aside. She was not his female to teach. That would be someone else's fun at some point. His little firecracker was more than enough.

It took him about an hour to get through the house, checking all the newly installed alarms. The new place would be very nice, he thought. Maybe he'd bring Beth out here for a treat. There were eight bedrooms, each with their own attached bathroom, a big kitchen, huge dining room plus a small owner's apartment. It wasn't furnished yet and he assumed that was why Miranda was there. He didn't know where the owner was but it didn't matter. He wrote up his report and went looking for Miranda to leave her a copy of it. He saw her standing, talking on her phone, with two people waiting to talk when she was done, he assumed. That was okay, he was in no hurry.

He walked to the big front window and stared out at the lake for a minute. He felt someone move behind him, so started to turn. Then he heard a voice that chilled him.

"Hello, Nick. I heard you were here. I'm Eli."

Nick took a deep breath and turned around slowly, blood running cold and his temper rising. Turning around he saw a remarkably nondescript man. No big bad monster, but yet, he knew he was. Or could be. Was. Would probably be again. Probably classically handsome, not that he cared. All he cared about was not punching him in the face.

"Hello, Eli," he said as calmly as he could manage. "Heard about you."

Eli nodded. "Imagine you have." He just stood there.

"So what can I do for you?"

"Figured you wanted to kill me," he said.

"Matter of fact, I do." Nick stared at him for a long minute controlling his urge, need, desire to put his hands around his throat and squeeze. Punch him hard. Kick him someplace very special.

"So why are you here?" he finally asked when Eli didn't say anything.

"I work here."

So much for bringing Beth here for a getaway.

"Not what I meant," he said, trying to stay as calm as possible. He found himself doing Beth's old trick of clenching her fists.

"In town, you mean? Why do you think I'm here?"

Nick clenched his fist and then forced himself to relax. He wasn't a barbarian. He wasn't going to lose his liberty or his job over this piece of scum.

"To cause Beth grief and anxiety and hurt her would be my first guess."

"Pretty much," he said and smiled in a way that really wanted to be knocked off his face. "Is it working?"

"Stay away from her," he said.

"Do you know what she did to me?"

"Do you know what you did to her?" Nick countered.

"Not as much as she deserved, She ruined my life. I want her to look over her shoulder every day of hers, knowing I can get to her anytime I want. I can't even see my kid anymore." He glared and Nick looked him in the eyes, knowing Beth saw these eyes as he attacked her.

"That's what happens when you beat up a helpless female."

"What she did to me was much much worse. Given the chance I'd do a better job of it."

Nick clenched his clipboard, wanting nothing more than to lunge at him. "That's mentally healthy," he said. "Stay away from her."

"I haven't come near her. But she knows I can and it's got to be eating her up."

He was not discussing Beth with this man. "Stay away

from her. Even better, move on. Find a better place to live and get therapy."

Eli shook his head. "Took me long enough to find her. Besides, I like this town. People are friendly, no one asks too many questions. There's a mousy little brunette, who used to be a smoking hot red head, slinking around here like she's hiding from the world. It entertains me to know I can make her sneak back in her hole at any time."

"Stay away from her." At least he hadn't seen her for a while, Nick realized. Beth's hair was red again. A gorgeous, burnished auburn. He loved it and knew he did not want Eli seeing it. Or her.

"I have been," Eli said. "And I'll continue to. Probably." He smirked in a way that made Nick so furious he had to count to ten.

"You better. For your own safety," he said very quietly.

It took everything Nick had inside him, to turn and walk away.

"No you aren't," Joni said. "That's ridiculous."

"No, it isn't," Beth said and took Nick's hand for comfort and support. "It is smart."

"You can't uproot your life and move to Missouri!" Joni reached for her phone and Beth assumed she was texting Hank. Were they on or off again? She didn't remember.

"Why is it smart? What makes it smart?"

"Well, for one thing, I don't have a life here. Other than you and Nick, I really don't have any friends."

"Sure you do. There's Jordyn and Ellie and—"

"Those are your friends," Beth interrupted. "I am not part of your circle."

Joni looked at her, and they both started as they heard the back door open.

"Just me," Hank called. "What's going on?" He walked into the room and looked around.

"Nick thinks he's moving Beth to Missouri! Tell them they are ridiculous."

"You are ridiculous," he repeated. "Why are they ridiculous? Nick, you got a job there? Beth can work from anywhere, I know."

Nick nodded. "There's an opening coming up at the fire station I used to work at. They say it's mine if I want it."

"Why are you doing this?" Joni said. "I don't understand."

"For Beth's safety," Nick said. "I talked to Eli a while back. She isn't safe here as long as he's around."

"What makes you think he can't find out where you moved?"

Beth looked at Nick. She'd been opposed to moving, to leaving Clearwater, but he'd explained it to her in a way that made sense. Hopefully, he could make Joni see it too. "I have a posse in Zephyrhills that I don't have here. I have four brothers, about ten cousins, a squad of people at the fire station who watched me grow up and grew up with me. I know everybody in town and they would protect my wife."

"Oh my God, are you getting married, too!"

Beth tried not to giggle at Joni's shock. Holding out her hand, she said, "He asked me last night and I said yes."

* * *

It had been magical. They'd driven out to the lake, to take a rather chilly walk on one of the paths while talking about the option of moving to Zephyrhills. She'd thought about it for a few days like he'd asked her to do. At first she outright rejected it. She wasn't running again. She'd done it once to no avail. It wasn't happening again.

He'd explained it wasn't running. It was a safety net he could provide her.

"So, are you going to spank me if I don't?" she asked him.

"Do you want me to spank you?"

"No!" she pouted. "It hurts."

"I'm confused. Isn't that the purpose?"

"I thought the purpose was a deterrent, or punishment, or you just flexing your Domly muscles."

"Well, I do like to flex my Domly muscles," he said. "But I only spank you if you need it."

"Why do you get to determine if I need it? Because you are the big bad wolf?"

"No, because I'm the knight in shining armor rescuing his damsel."

"You are ridiculous is what you are," she said.

"Yes, but I'm the ridiculous one with the paddle," he said, and pulled out a soft leather thing from his jacket pocket that she stared at.

"Oh, no!" She started to back away. "It's too cold!"

He laughed. "Too cold for a spanking? I'm just planning to warm you up. I'm a helper, too."

"Nope, nope, nope," she said and shook her head.

He pulled her over to a bench and said, "Drop your pants."

"No! It's cold! I wasn't bad!"

"I'll warm you up and no one said you were. Now, do as you were told."

"I don't want to." She crossed her arms.

"I don't imagine you do," he said, and grinned at her, "considering you're going to be kicking and squalling in a few minutes. But, on the up side..."

"Up side?"

"Your butt will be warm."

"Great," she muttered and for some reason her chilled fingers went to her jeans snap and she undid them and slowly pulled the zipper down, but couldn't bring herself to drop them.

"Now," he said, and slapped his thigh with the leather paddle. "Before I get too impatient, and take it out on that cute butt."

"Like you aren't going to anyway," she complained but finally did as she was told and tossed herself over his lap. "I'm cold! Your fault!"

"Won't be long," he assured her and shifted her weight. She could feel the paddle trace across her bare bottom and shivered from cold or anticipation she wasn't sure. Then yelped as the first strike landed. "I do love how pink the leather makes your bottom and how it wiggles and bounces around when I smack it."

"Well, as long as you are happy," she said. "Ow!"

"Oh, did that get your attention?"

"It did! Ow! Dang! Nick! I'm warm! You can stop!"

"Yet, I don't think I will," he said and she wiggled under four more swats.

"Ow!" Beth felt her voice rise. "No more! I'll be good!"

"Good and warm," he agreed and she started kicking and wiggling and twisting to get off his lap but he didn't stop. Didn't even seem to notice and she didn't like it one bit. He should at least be bothered by her distress. Wasn't relieving that stress what knights did? Or at least notice that she was doing her best to get away because it hurt!

"Ouch! I'm done now! Nice and warm! Please!"

"Oh, a little bit more, I think," he said and didn't stop. Her bottom stung and hurt and she had to put her hand back to stop the pain, block it, slow it, redirect it, something! Anything! Of course he grabbed both her wrists as he often did and held her hands together, making her feel helpless and a little out of control.

"I'm sorry! I'll be good!" she shrieked, not caring if anyone in the woods heard her.

"How good?" he asked, pausing and she sighed in relief, wishing he'd let go of her hands so she could rub her sore bottom.

"As good as you want me to be!" she told him, hoping she sounded sincere.

"I want you to be this good," he said and she felt something slip on her finger. Then he pulled her up and stood her in front of him while she looked at the most beautiful diamond she'd ever seen in her life, forgetting about her pants around her knees. "Will my well-paddled red head marry me and make me happy and have the need to carry a flogger in my pocket for the rest of my life?"

"Did you seriously just propose to me while I'm half naked in the woods?" she grumbled pulling up her pants before the heat in her bottom dissipated. That felt better.

"I did," he said, looking at her while she zipped up her jeans and winced. "But only after I gave you what you needed, which I will always do. Well?"

"Well, what – oh, well, yes, Nick Kinkirk I will marry you!" With that she flung herself into his arms. "But my next proposal better not come with a sore bottom."

He swatted her. "Better not be another one."

"Darn right," she'd said.

———

Now she looked at Joni. "Married in his hometown with his family and friends there, moving there. You are the only friend I have in town, and Mom and Sydney will fly in here or there. All Nick's family and friends are there, so it makes sense. It will be nice for you to have the house to yourself and no reason to be afraid or worry," she said. "I'll be safe there."

"Damn right you will," Nick said and pulled her close. "For the rest of our lives. Now you girls have a wedding to plan and Hank and I are going to have a beer."

They headed to the backyard and Beth looked at Joni. "You going to be okay here alone?"

She nodded. "Yeah, and I'm pretty sure I won't be alone long."

Beth watched her eyes follow Hank out of the room and felt pretty sure Joni might be right. If Hank was half as smart as her fiancé.

She smiled at Joni, her sister and best friend in the world, 'Will you be my maid of honor?"

Epilogue

Joni leaned against Hank as he drove the big, rented truck back home. They'd just been in Zephyrhills for a week. Helped move Nick and Beth in to their new house and then attended the wedding. She was ready to be home, but... "Are we really leaving her there?"

"Are you going to cry again?" Hank asked, reaching in his pocket.

"I might," she grabbed the tissue he offered. "It just feels wrong to be so far away from her."

"I met all of Nick's family. I spent time with them and talked to them. She's going to be safe. Dropped in at the police station with him and we made sure they know what's going on. Nick has friends there too. She's going to be in a bubble of safety."

"I know." Joni tried not to complain. She wasn't complaining. She was rightfully worried about her sister. It was her job. "But I've done it for three years now. It feels like I'm neglecting my duties or something."

"Joni, you aren't her mother. She has a husband and a new

126

family who will take care of her. You can take care of you now."

"I'm fine," she snapped at him. He could be so sweet, but so insufferable. It was a long way to get back to Clearwater though, so she didn't want to pick a fight with him just yet. It would happen though, she knew, before they got too close to home. And he'd just let it. Let her. It had been very sweet of him to take a week out of his life to help her family though. How many people would do that? She grabbed her phone from her pocket and texted Beth. *"Are you doing fine?"*

"All good, don't worry. Going out to dinner with some of Nick's friends."

Joni sighed and put her phone up.

"What's wrong?" Hank asked.

"Nothing," she said, trying her best to keep her tone civil.

"Why don't you try to take a nap?" he said. "It will be about three more hours till we get home."

"Yeah, a nap is what I need," she said, leaning back in her seat. Suddenly, he was all she had. Well, not really. He wasn't hers. He seemed happy with their on-again, off-again relationship. She wasn't. But she wasn't sure what she wanted.

He was perfect. The man was literally perfect. It was so annoying.

He taught middle school like she did, he was a Master Gardener, which she wasn't. He baked. He cooked. He volunteered to coach Peewee football on top of coaching the junior high team that was part of his job. He was writing a freaking novel. Who does that? He could fix things, he walked his elderly neighbor's dog, and never lost his temper. How could anyone measure up to that?

And yet, he did nothing when she threw tantrums, or jumped out of the car, or stormed out of a dinner. Nothing! Just let her be for a few hours or days, brought her candy, flowers or chocolate and considered it over. And she always let him back in. What was with that? She was tired of living like that, but he seemed to want to do nothing about it.

———————

Hank looked over at Joni as she seemed to drift off to sleep. Or fumed. He wasn't sure which. It didn't matter. He needed to get her home before she jumped out of the truck and ran away. Keeping her safe was important, even though it was Beth who'd been in danger. He'd keep a close eye on her, though, just in case the scum bag lurking around town decided not to take Beth leaving well. They hadn't announced it but word got around. Scumbag Eli's new girlfriend, Miranda, her brother Ben was engaged to Jordyn, who was Joni's good friend. It seemed a far connection but word got around. He needed to keep an eye on Joni and figure out what they were doing. They'd been on and off again for a couple years now. For a genius, as his sister Ellie told him sometimes, he sure could be dumb.

He'd gone to Nick's bachelor party with Nick's brothers and friends while they were in Nick's hometown for the wedding. They'd all taught him a few things about handling women. He'd known these things, but really, while these things were a part of him, part of how he actually felt, he also knew you just couldn't do that anymore. Women were equal, more than equal, he knew. That wasn't the issue. The issue was Joni didn't seem happy getting away with the things she did. If she wasn't, then why did she keep doing the same things repeatedly that made her, and him, upset?

While she wasn't a true redhead like her sister Beth, or Moriah who worked at the bakery on the square she had a short temper, except when she was teaching. There she had a limitless supply of patience. Any other time and the woman would go off and sometimes he didn't even know what caused it. But she was soon going to find out what cured it.

Megan McCoy

Megan McCoy lives in the heartland of America, surrounded by corn, soybean fields and hot guys on tractors. At home, she's raising kids, Chinese Cresteds and poodles, training them all with a tender hand and heart, while saving her sternness for the alpha males in her books. Getting up at three in the morning to write leaves her time for a few hobbies - gardening, canning, bike riding, bread baking and taking in strays.

Don't miss these exciting books by Megan McCoy and Blushing Books!

Clearwater Romance series
The Wife He Wanted
The Wife He Adored
The Wife He Needed
The Wife He Protected

Hometown Love series
Don't Mess with Jess
Hannah and Hawk
Totally Tori
Kelly's Haven
Hometown Love Collection

Her Choice series
His Firecracker
The Dilemma

The City Girl
Her Choice, Always
Her Choice Forever

South Dakota Dreams series
Stormy's Trouble
Talia's Time
Wynter's Waif
Wynter's Wife
Sailor's Search
South Dakota Dreams Collection

Along Came Jones Series
Sebastian
Hank
Logan and Ronnie
Logan's Contract
Along Came Jones Collection

Single Titles
Two Weeks of Joy
An Old-Fashioned Relationship
Hard Wired Desires
Quinn's Comeuppance

Anthologies
12 Naughty Days of Christmas 2016
12 Naughty Days of Christmas 2017
12 Naughty Days of Christmas 2020

Audio-Books
An Old-Fashioned Relationship

Connect with Megan McCoy

www.meganmccoy.com

Blushing Books

Blushing Books is the oldest eBook publisher on the web. We've been running websites that publish steamy romance and erotica since 1999, and we have been selling eBooks since 2003. We have free and promotional offerings that change weekly, so please do visit us at http://www.blushingbooks.com/free.

Blushing Books Newsletter

Please join the Blushing Books newsletter
to receive updates & special promotional offers.
You can also join by using your mobile phone:
Just text BLUSHING to 22828.

Every month, one new sign up via text messaging will receive
a $25.00 Amazon gift card, so sign up today!